# Santiago's Way

# Patricia Laurent
# Santiago's Way

Translated from the Spanish by Geoff Hargreaves

Peter Owen
London and Chester Springs

PETER OWEN PUBLISHERS
73 Kenway Road, London SW5 0RE

Peter Owen books are distributed in the USA by
Dufour Editions Inc., Chester Springs, PA 19425-0007

English language edition first published in Great Britain 2004
by Peter Owen Publishers

Translated from the Spanish *El Camino de Santiago*
© Patricia Laurent 2000
English translation © Geoff Hargreaves 2004

ISBN 0 7206 1190 3

A catalogue record for this book is available from
the British Library

Printed and bound in Great Britain
by MPG Books Ltd, Bodmin, Cornwall

# Prologue

I should make it clear at the start that three things menace my well-being: a sense of abandonment, the sight of a cradle that ceases its rocking and a sudden onset of darkness. If I listen to torrents of water I am also filled with dread. I can recall no worse experience than taking a bath in the ocean. My recurrent nightmare is of an enormous wave that surges to a height of twelve feet or more but never comes crashing down.

The rest of the terrors, as indecipherable as flashes of lightning that curdle the blood, belong to Santiago, the intruder who invaded my body when I first opened my veins.

The fourteenth year of my existence was the saddest I'd ever known. Not so much because of the scandal in my family, somewhat so because of my failed suicide attempt but, principally, as a result of a hallucination that threatened my reason.

Before Santiago found refuge in the currents of my blood, he used to circle around me. Invisible, he breathed hotly on my shoulder. He pestered me, behaving like the very opposite of a guardian angel, as he waited for my moment of greatest weakness to unite his missing dimension with mine. While he was tracing out the topography of my encephalic routes, which harbour him today, his proximity distracted and disturbed me, forcing me to stand guard in case he stole all the memories I had stored up from those early years when Mina and I thrust our way past life's rules and limitations with the impetuous enthusiasm of humming-birds.

Lord and master of his dwelling places, he now guards, inside his intricate web of caves, a multitude of photos designed to provoke shame and repentence as well as movies he plays over and over on the screen of his disgust. In a leaky canoe he travels along the currents of my being. The broader the river, the further he infiltrates up the white-water rapids.

His quickest shortcut lies through dreams. He opens up galleries in them and exhibits there images of my life: a ruined building floating on slimy waters, a lover who changes into a metallic-blue wasp that deposits its eggs in the abdomen of a paralysed tarantula, my mother who transforms into a toboggan of stone.

I intuit his presence curled up on some neuronal mound. 'I am the sole mistress of my body,' I assert defiantly.

He argues back that we are one and the same.

Out of a doughy mixture of slippery facts I try to reconstruct Mina. She is still out there somewhere, in the indigo-blue, past deep wells, wide lagoons and abandoned buildings. For years now Santiago has been hiding her behind this menacing landscape. He annuls my optic nerve so that he won't even be seen to approach the tunnel that leads to her.

He refuses to contribute from his hoard of metaphors and syntax the language I need to imagine Mina, the alternative to him.

'That would be going too far,' he snaps peevishly.

I calm him down with a short selection from Mozart. I offer my body a shot of dark-roast coffee, while I speak of the horror of being unable to tell a convincing story.

Sufficiently appeased, Santiago finally agrees to let me have enough vocabulary to ensure a reader's understanding. He will act as a faithful mirror to my rudimentary alphabet. He will observe, comprehend, assert, and I can tell my story. But he is afraid of being judged too harshly. In fact, he would prefer not to continue at all with this compromising act of cooperation.

# 1

To prove that he has always inhabited my body, Santiago flourishes a packet of photos taken from the time of my birth up to the moment when I tried to declare my independence from him. Like a professional gambler, he fans out the photos and selects one at random.

Here my father is drinking with his mates. It isn't clear whether they are in the living-room or the kitchen. He calls on his children, one by one, to perform the tricks he has taught us. Because I have almost no appetite, my body is extremely skinny, and my performance consists of spinning around on my axis while he blows on me. I pretend to be trapped in a whirlwind until I fall and hit the floor like a plank. His friends laugh and clap. Intoxicated by success, I retire to the bedroom where my older brothers and sister are planning mutiny. The ringleader is Javier. At this time he is twelve years old and he fancies Consuelo, the daughter of my father's friend Garces. Javier's party piece (his inability to refuse to perform this babyish trick drives him wild) consists of simply twirling his hand from front to back. With the palm facing forwards, he sings, 'I have a little hand.' Then he turns the back of the hand to his audience and sings, as if they were all two-year-olds, 'I don't have a little hand, because it's fallen to pieces.'

Santiago possesses a whole collection of such photos, slides and transparencies that he will go on showing to me over the course of our sickly union. He is I and I am he, he claims. All the rest is just astral sleight of hand. There is no way I can treat him lightly, and he warns me to watch out for those moments of throbbing wildness when I act like a person in a dream, totally out of control. Any deviation from the norm makes him nervous. He assures me that my problems are the predictable result of a pathological compulsion. He urges me to read a good book on health maintenance.

Why do I drink so much? Smoke so much? It all ends in dreadful hallucinations. How can I hope to achieve physical harmony when I pollute my body all the time?

# 2

For ever floating, unable to reach land and change into my real self, I rehearse the gestures of other bodies: how they eat and laugh, how they carry their books to school. I imitate my classmates. I tread in the footsteps of neighbours when I go to the corner shop. I learn what I'm supposed to do when it rains: spin around with my mouth open and catch raindrops on my tongue. It's as if I explore level ground with the passion of a hill-climber. With my eyes half open I practise staring at the sun for long periods.

My sister and my brothers were excellent models for what a body could be. I filched sketches of behaviour from them and signed them with my own name. I stole their love stories and made myself their protagonist. I faked the musculature of my brother Alejandro and had fights with other girls on the strength of an insult or a laugh.

The one thing I could never copy was their way of really understanding things. I lived with a defect in that area. When it came to comprehending the rules of a game I battled in vain.

A marble, for example, is something you hold in your fingers. You look at it. You rub it between your hands and warm it up, so you can enjoy its round little body. Then you give it away to somebody or other.

No, they tell me. That's not it. No and no again. Marbles are for hiding in a drawer. I can take them out when I've finished a page of handwriting practice. I knock them against other marbles and wait until somebody tells me if I've won or lost, because I never figured out when I was doing it right. I trusted my siblings' sense of fair play. They were the judges. They pronounced the verdict.

Sometimes I thought I had a talent for logical reasoning. But it was a guaranteed disaster if I took the initiative.

This photo of the neighbourhood where I grew up shows the Gonzalez kids, a clan of five brothers and sisters. One fewer than our six. I never understood the reason, but we and they hated each other's guts. At least that was simple. Don't say hello to them. Don't address a single word to them. And most of all – this was absolutely clear – never make them a present of a marble.

Hatred. That's the way it is. No rhyme, no reason. It's like grass. It grows without needing attention. It feeds itself. It springs up on its own.

At last, here was something I understood. I liked the idea of seeing myself aligned with my family in a battle. My brothers and sister used to have fun drawing up maps of how we could bypass the Gonzalez kids. Applause and cheers were in order when one of us returned unscathed from a trip to buy tortillas.

Then the inevitable occurred. We all bumped into one another in the square. Glances were exchanged. Spit flew out of mouths. Curses followed. The long-expected war cry rang out.

When the battle began, I found myself without an adversary. I was supernumerary to the engagement. It was then that I took the initiative. The Gonzalez kids had brought a playful puppy with them. This was my opportunity. I delivered kicks to my canine foe. I grabbed it by the tail, whirled it around and thwacked it against a wire-mesh fence. Stunned by my action, both warring bands stopped fighting. Still sweating with hatred, they both turned on me, raining down blows.

Afterwards, my own siblings – in other words, my own team, the army composed of my closest relatives – refused to speak to me. Finally, I understood that there were rules, even in hatred, that could not be broken. After several hours of being given the cold shoulder I pretended I had seen the point, and I was forgiven.

# 3

While Santiago was circling around my dreams Mina set up house in me with a bang. Together we explored land and terrifying sea. Sounds and tastes. The fireworks of an exploding spirit.

My mother sent me to buy tortillas. I had to cross a square shaded by almond trees, under which stood an abandoned kiosk. As I returned with a kilo of tortillas a man spoke to me. He was seated on a bench. He showed no sign of possessing a Santiago, and his Mina, like mine nowadays, was concealed behind shattered fragments of memory. He was a typical beggar, dressed in blackened clothes that had once been beige. Chewing-gum was stuck to his long hair. His eyes were small, but, in spite of their opaqueness, they had the sharp look of a rat's. He called out to me as I passed. I headed towards him quite naturally, for human beings did not figure in my list of phobias.

He asked me for a tortilla. As I unwrapped the package he slipped his hand under the skirt of my school uniform. I detached the first tortilla and observed the steam that arose from the one beneath it. The beggar took the tortilla with one hand. The other, in the shade of an almond tree, pushed aside my panties and began to stroke me. Before his hand got any further inside Mina and I held a conversation. Why was he touching my pee-pee? That was what we were going to find out. Mina assured me everything was fine. The man had this small need. We stayed where we were. The man took me by the hand and sat me down on the bench beside him. I mentioned that he had no Santiago to guide him, because I don't recall his being worried somebody was going to see him. Eating tortillas, Mina and I discovered the delights of touch. She took control of the situation. Inside me things turned into a ball of light, then, with the help of the man's finger and the dilated clitoris, everything exploded into hundreds of tiny suns.

Santiago now searches for this picture of the plaza, which, according to him, he photographed in minute detail.

'To begin with,' he says, 'your mother, because of that inattentiveness of hers that we are so familiar with, forgets how little you are to be crossing the avenue by yourself, on your way to the square. Here you can see this white car that had to brake to avoid killing you. Once we get to the square we have forgotten all about the errand. We settle down to study ants that are pulling pieces off the blood-red shells of fallen almonds. While we are sitting in the sand under the almond trees, the beggar, who is really none other than the lollipop-seller, comes by and asks what you are doing. Tears spring to your eyes, for you suddenly realize you have lost the money and will get a beating, so you make him a despairing answer. He offers to give you a coin. He takes a shining peso out of his pocket. It is blindingly bright in the midday sun. At this point you approach him. Screened by his lollipop cart, he slides his hands under your panties and strokes you with his moistened finger. This other photo here of your internal events shows the explosion of the sun – but look, see how dark it gets afterwards.'

'I lost Mina in that darkness.'

'The lollipop-seller fits your hand to his hardened penis. Of course, you don't know what to do. When you come back with the kilo of tortillas he intercepts you again. He asks you for a tortilla and says he will expect you the next day. So you lost more than a coin that day. Here are the photos of the days when you are crying and kicking, so as not to be sent to the tortilla shop. You say you are afraid to go because of the Gonzalez kids, although the older ones, the most belligerent, are in school at that hour. Reluctantly, Lilia has to take on the job of fetching the tortillas. She threatens to get her revenge on you.'

# 4

I never ceased to be amazed by my sister Lilia. She was only eleven months my senior, but she understood everything, from bathing in the ocean to the right way to combine her outfits. She had elegant manners and always won top academic honours. She was born charming. She knew how to dance and even had a seductive smile with a slight tilt to it. My mouth practised various sorts of smiles but to no avail: they all looked like scrunched-up spiders.

In primary school I tried to dance. I asked the teacher, Miss Cuquita, to include me in one of the concerts she put on for Mother's Day. She had fond memories of my sister's talent and gave me the starring role. After a few rehearsals she regretted it. She then put me in the chorus line, as a partner in one of the numerous pairs. She regretted that, too. My body couldn't remember the dance: it ground to a halt at the back of the stage, its eyes fixed on the rest of the swirling chorus. To top things off, I was dribbling. The boy assigned as my partner made the situation worse by refusing to dance with my clumsy body. Miss Cuquita chastized him for his bad manners. To console me she gave me a red caramel lollipop, sat me down on the stage steps and promised to include me in some other dance.

That never happened.

Maybe because of my lack of logic I forgive easily. But Santiago, that intruder in my body, driven by power, pride and desire, does not. I am supposed to recognize that his growing willingness to forgive is an indispensable element in his struggle to maintain my health, but I now see it is a ruse to stay in control of me for years to come. Although I know he feels humiliated by the need to forgive, he did start to learn how to do it after the incident with the lollipop-seller. But he made that concession only to gain my favour. He wanted to persuade me that he had not usurped the places he occupies in my body.

So why all the bad feeling? Because he cannot overlook my attempts at loving. I was a lover from my earliest years, before he came to dominate me, when Mina and I lived in ecstasies of discovery. Together we loved a body that no Santiago controlled, as we had loved that beggar's. His name was Cheese-Buns, because he sold bread and cheese outside the school. I was in my third year at the primary school. He and I had something in common: dribbling.

I approached him with the burning need that my body had learned to recognize that noon in the square. I made my advance little by little, because otherwise Cheese-Buns would let out a howl and run off in panic. Sometimes, when he ran, he left his basket behind, and I used to pick it up.

One day I followed him street after street, until I finally found him hiding behind a tree. Once I was close to him I stood looking at him for a long time. I gave him back his basket and the merchandise he had abandoned. After several attempts I managed to stroke his face. Then I licked his neck. He laughed outrageously and dribbled uncontrollably. I showed him some photos from my brother Javier's anatomy textbook. They depicted two adolescents with their lower bellies dissected, and one of them had its testicles showing in order to explain the reproductive process. With the two of us hidden inside an asbestos drainage pipe on some waste ground we dribbled as we touched each other.

I taught him to stroke me gently, because at first he hurt me. Mina had been controlling the explosion of the suns but, inexplicably, she disappeared, leaving behind her a sickening dizziness followed by a sensation of flying through a blue void.

Soon it became impossible to see Cheese-Buns any more. He had started crossing the pavement to the windows of my classroom. He didn't care that the teacher and my classmates were present. He would let out a howl and pull out his penis. Then he would throw buns against the glass of the windows, trying to get me to come out of the school. The headmaster phoned somebody and they took Cheese-Buns away for good.

# 5

I have discovered that alcohol fumes can scare off Santiago like magic. When I get drunk I experience a rebirth of childlike love, the sort I felt for Cheese-Buns. I love fearlessly, recklessly, with the shameless need to take desire to the verge of the abyss, where the flesh can no longer go. Once my body has spilled itself out, all limp, Santiago cannot navigate through the diverted traffic routes and scrambled brain signals.

With my inner landscape in flames and the telephone lines tangled, I have often experienced love for people I would abandon at dawn. Afterwards, Santiago would emerge, bursting with indignation, bustling out from his caves and claiming I was ruining myself with the tin-pan serenades of promiscuity, with unwelcome bodily fluids and the serious risk of infection.

He assures me that avoiding the Seven Deadly Sins is the key to good health. Loss of health would mean disaster for me. The control of gluttony, envy, pride, lust, sloth, anger and greed is his greatest obsession.

He knows how dangerous it would be for my body – our body – to push those sins to the limit. I tend to go overboard with gluttony, sloth and anger. The rest of them – lust now included – lie dormant, thanks to my natural indifference to material possessions, the decline in my physical allure and the absence of any exceptional intelligence that might tempt us to arrogance.

Gluttony is my name for anything I put into myself via my mouth, from tobacco smoke through culinary delicacies to the inevitable wine. Sloth adheres to my body as firmly as any of my extremities. My blood pressure is low and any temperature above twenty-six degrees centigrade makes my eyes and shoulders droop and leaves my knees sagging.

I control my anger the way an AA member controls the urge to drink. I have been doing it since the time I waged war – emotional, mental and physical – on Vicente, a boyfriend who refused to end our relationship.

I was incapable of loving him. How could I have loved him, burdened with my baggage of frights and terrors? Back then I still had not understood that Santiago and I were not identical. I thought that rancorous bitterness was a part of my spiritual makeup.

At that time, however, I had realized that I could not love by taking everything from Mina and nothing from Santiago. The ideal was to enjoy a dual-natured love like a grey-toned kiss shared in the last gleam of daylight, when day and night are meeting and, for a brief moment, there beams out a ray of subtle light that guards the secret of their balance. So I failed when I aimed to confine Santiago to his caves, hoping that I could love solely with the moist intensity that had guided my nose to the tunnel of Mina.

Those failures taught me to understand things. Those various wounds. Those several jokes. I can still hear Santiago's reproaches.

'It's not right for you to go down the street hugging people. And you shouldn't be kissing the boys from the basketball team. You have to restrain yourself. Otherwise nobody's going to love you. Look at that nice boy from your school. He prefers a quiet girl: one who smiles demurely and doesn't cackle with laughter; one who doesn't lift her legs when she gets a fit of the giggles. Look at her sort of shoes, patent leather with gold laces, and then at your horrible football boots that used to belong to your brother Alejandro.'

Thanks to Santiago, lord and master of my mind, whose sceptre is my fear of rejection, I got the message.

From that day on the warm, soft breezes of Mina were excluded from my body. Santiago explained the Plan to me: 'If you like a man, you must give him only homoeopathic doses of love.'

That's what I did. The boy I had loved in vain in primary school, Guillermo, I saw again in high school. My eyes were now full of mystery. I had been initiated into the wisdom of never showing emotion. The Plan worked. This time Guillermo fell for me, heavily. But there was nothing I could do to help him. My breast was hermetically sealed.

I'm not going to claim that all men fell victim to Santiago's Plan. But some certainly did. As seductions got more complicated, my hermetic mystery didn't prove sufficient. We were in desperate need of a more mature public persona, so Santiago came up with the idea of creating an almost perfect replica of Mina: sincere, warm and genuine.

Winning these battles of non-love brings us to the photo of my twenty-third year when I embarked on a love-war and unleashed a long-repressed anger that cost me half my emotional and physical health, which I sometimes take care of and sometimes listlessly neglect.

## 6

My hair has always been long and thick. I am tall. My face is rather odd, half-way towards a Picasso portrait. My breasts never developed. They are like a doll's: small, round, with the nipple so pink as to be nearly invisible. My hips are broad but not disgustingly so. Still, I have to watch my carbohydrate intake so that they don't get out of hand. I walk with my shoulders hunched. Before Santiago invaded me, I grew so quickly that I wanted to hide my body. After his Plan was instituted, I struggled in vain to straighten my spine into a tall, spindly column worthy of a supermodel. Santiago and I soon found ourselves bored with easy prey. We wanted a challenge, and Vicente roused an instant attraction in us. Of athletic build, with round, yellow eyes, he was possessed by an extremely seductive Santiago. His IQ was far above average and he had the haughty pride that is justifiable only in those who believe they have found out the truth about life.

At supper he drank only one glass of wine. He didn't smoke at all. He didn't eat fat and was a fanatical bodybuilder. I ought to have had misgivings about his ambitions, for anyone who strives to live and show strength beyond his natural limits must be thinking of himself as Nietzsche's Superman, that wild caricature of the Antichrist.

In my opinion, forgiveness is the noblest of all Christian teachings, but Superman, a being from an alien planet, is incapable of it. Instead of turning the other cheek and bringing violence to an end, he is a living fury who ends up enjoying the power of his role as the sole hero of Metropolis.

Vicente's vanity, like the Superman's, had the saving grace of keeping him away from far worse addictions. Anybody who wants to live beyond his natural term merits all my distrust. Predators and consumers that we are, the best we can do for the planet is to die early in the hope of minimizing its decline. That's what I know now, but at twenty-three years of age I still regarded humanity with a certain ingenuousness.

In the first of Santiago's photos taken of that encounter, Vicente is playing chess, a game of suspect sanity that combines cool logic with the fervour of a crusade. The poor fool who plays it as a means to an end never knows when it becomes an end in itself. But I have to admit admiration for the men who renounce the search for industrial, cultural, political or social power to misuse their warlike instincts across a tiny board on a café table.

Vicente was an excellent chess player. According to Plan Santiago, I was required to demonstrate an intelligence that bordered on the anti-feminine but without stepping over the line. With my mouth half-open and my eyes wide with astonishment, I was to act as if profoundly impressed by the clever things men said to me.

The Plan was getting progressively more difficult. I had to achieve financial and social independence, to pursue projects that had nothing to do with marriage and to develop athletic abilities, at least in aerobics. But one quality Santiago insisted I acquire was beyond me: enthusiasm. By that term I also mean optimism, *joie de vivre*, faith, hope and serenity.

Sooner or later any lover capable of playing several games of simultaneous chess was bound to see through the farcical surface of my humanity. I have already mentioned that, as a cerebral weakling with regard to logic and method, I managed early on to imitate the lives of my siblings, that of Lilia in particular, but I could not pull it off after I reached the age of thirteen. Anyone can copy, but forgery is an art. Up to thirteen I could fake certain qualities, talents and signs of intelligence, but then Lilia sped off in directions I simply did not comprehend. Like Darwin, I could not find the missing link, the thing that suddenly catapulted her into womanhood, into being a professional worker, a lover, a wife, a mother.

The photos that relate to my life after fourteen – that's to say, after my suicide attempt and the invasion by Santiago – are a series of variations based on the Plan.

First photograph. With some university texts under my arm, I arrive at the Wormwood Café where chess is played. I encounter the feline eyes of Vicente. They look at me without looking at me. I have a coffee and smoke a cigarette. I open the most baffling book I have ever laid eyes on, *Integral Applied Equations*. It was part of Santiago's Plan to have me enrolled in the School of Engineering. I peer at the book. I stroke it. The integrals have symbols that look like snakes rearing their heads. At the back of my brain arises a question: will the day ever dawn when I understand all this? I check my watch. I am waiting for a good-natured friend who is going to explain to me the meaning of the snakes. When I am totally lost in incomprehension, Vicente speaks to me:

'Integrals?'

The seduction gets under way. Vicente already has two engineering degrees. He is single, thirty-one years old. He is an independent consultant to refrigeration companies. The last thing I want to tell him is that I've no idea what integrals are about, let alone all that mess of geometry, algebra and differentials. Instead, I tell him that I, too, play chess. Santiago unleashes a vigorous attack with a panache almost worthy of Capablanca. We don't beat Vicente but we impress him.

Second photograph. Vicente invites me to his apartment. I can't accept it. Not if we are playing love-chess. It would be like accepting Queen's Gambit and holding on to the poisoned pawn.

Third photograph. I go back to the Wormwood Café. Vicente winks at me. He is showing off. He flaunts himself as he checkmates his opponent. While I wait for him to finish playing for the day, he recommends me to others as an opponent. A long-haired man with glasses challenges me. I whip him. Vicente is so proud. He invites me out to dinner.

Sitting opposite me, he asks me questions. I give him half-answers. I retain a halo of mystery.

In the *septum lucidum* there is a series of photos and blurred transparencies that covers the progress of the romance: playing tennis, movies, Chinese food, Greek food, Italian food, jokes, raucous laughs (including those forbidden by Santiago), holding hands, excellent wine and a kiss.

My father has been dead for five years when I move in with Vicente. My mother raises an appalling fuss, but her own indiscretions undermine her protests. She wants me to follow Lilia's shining example and make something of my life.

'You should be glad I'm still alive,' I tell her.

## 7

This photo of Vicente has another stuck to it. It refers to the Case of Felicitas. They are together in the album, because they are connected by squabbling, the desire for power and its defeat.

Felicitas was in primary school with me. We did the fifth year together. She was not very bright, but she had a charisma that I didn't have and that I was later supposed to practise as part of Plan Santiago.

We are both the same height. She wears her hair in long braids and she has gleaming black eyes. Her complexion is white, although she has Indian features. Every thirty seconds she spits and grabs her skirt to her crotch as if she wants to pee. Her laugh is ear-splitting. Maybe that's where I picked up my own unappealing cackle. She is a great friend of Cleotilde, the only girl in the class who feels comfortable with fractions and logical problems. Felicitas is also a first-rate volleyball player. She curses a lot and threatens to beat up members of the opposing team. We are all scared of her anger. Miss Graciela, the teacher, adores her. She asks her to clean the blackboard and make a list of the girls who talk when they shouldn't. She is fair to her friends. She protects them. She was the only one who was suspicious of me when, two years earlier, Cheese-Buns used to peer through the windows. The others all believed he had fallen for my pale complexion and empty eyes without any sort of provocation. But Felicitas tackled me about it in the bathroom.

'You were seen with him in the drainage-pipe,' she said. I kept on washing my hands as if she were a ghost. 'I'm talking to you,' she insisted, and hit me on the back. I looked at her, pleading and afraid. She lowered her eyelids as if dropping a curtain of complicity: she was never going to reveal my secret. I shook the water off my hands and left the bathroom. For two years she did not re-enter my life.

In this photo it is break time between classes, and I am not alone. I have Martha with me, a timid creature who follows me all over the playground. She used to attend a convent school, but after her father went bankrupt she ended up in our neighbourhood school. She still carries traces of her middle-class background. She brings to school some excellent lunches of fruit juices and baked ham. She invites me to share them. Removing ourselves from the general hubbub and the ball games, we eat together in the shade of the playground's only mesquite tree. I tell her stories, ones that, as I admitted earlier, I stole from my siblings. I show her sketches I pilfered from my brother Luis. I tell her I am brilliant at chess and maths. This lie leads to a major problem. Martha is not only hopeless at maths but, because she still dresses and behaves in a middle-class way, nobody but me ever speaks to her.

I circumvent my mathematical ineptitude with help from Floripez, a gentle-spirited mountain of a girl who makes supernatural efforts to understand the world of numbers. Floripez receives help from Cleotilde, who will help only her and Felicitas. Floripez then tutors me, and in my turn, in exchange for company and delicious sandwiches, I explain things to Martha.

I should have accepted my lowly position in this chain with proper humility. But no. One day Felicitas is sick. Her group of friends is standing around chatting about a horror film. There are nine or ten of them, all with characters like Felicitas's but with less of the bully. I ask them about Felicitas. They ignore me, except one.

'She's sick,' she answers.

'Sick?' I say. 'I bet she is. You should have seen us two yesterday, tangling outside Doña Delia's shop.' I now have their full attention.

'You two had a fight?'

'Too right we did,' I say. 'Well, you know me. I don't like to fight, but if you come looking for one, you'll get one.' I got the expression from a movie. 'I don't know why she picked on me,' I continue, 'I didn't want to fight, but a gal's gotta do what a gal's gotta do.' I spit. The girls are all ears. They stand back and give me room to tell the rest of my story. I describe in gory detail my fictitious fight with Felicitas. 'I forced her to run away.' The group stares at me, astounded. 'Yes, I did,' I assure them. 'It happened outside the shop. She's so jealous of me. I was buying this hair-clip.' I show them a clip I had looted from my mother's knick-knack box in her jewellery drawer and smuggled out between my schoolbooks. 'Felicitas called me a bad name.'

'What name?' one of them asks.

'Slut.' It is the first time in my life the word has passed my lips.

They all hush, comprehending the gravity of the situation. That afternoon I enjoy heroic status. I tell Martha how I routed Felicitas. I also tell my sister Lilia. She is horrified. Then she says that if I don't clip her toenails for her she'll tell Dad. I clip her nails, basking in her admiration. Lilia, like Cleotilde, does not need physical courage. Her understanding saves her. Now in the sixth year of school, she is consulted, like a great oracle, on all things logical – but even she regards me with awe.

You might think I'd learn a lesson from all this but, as the next photo shows, I had no grasp of power struggles.

The next day Felicitas returns to school. From eight o'clock until ten everything proceeds as normal. Now I am asking myself: what was I thinking? Did I imagine that Felicitas wasn't going to find out? Or was it a form of suicide?

Two minutes into the break somebody tells Felicitas the story of the hair-clip. I have just enough time to dip into the lunch Martha has brought me. I am in mid-chew when I see Felicitas and her group of friends heading my way. I have one shred of pride left. I could have fled and skulked behind the skirts of one of the teachers who adore Lilia, but I stand my ground.

Felicitas does not ask me if I said it or not. She grabs me by my long hair. She dumps me on the soil and gravel of the playground. She drags me around the mesquite tree. She isn't stupid: to drag me over to where the ball games are played would attract the attention of the teachers. I cling to the roots of my hair to reduce the pain. But having my hands on my hair means my chin gets scraped on the ground. After several circuits of the tree Felicitas kicks me in the ribs, between my jawbone and my neck, on my legs. She is making her point that she is not ready to relinquish her ranking in the pecking order. She would have gone a lot further if it had not been for Floripez.

'Leave her alone,' says the mountain of a girl. Felicitas is reluctant to let go of my hair. Floripez makes a fighting gesture and Felicitas releases me, spitting on my back as she goes.

'You see?' Floripez tells me from the furthest shadows of the photo. 'That's what you get for being a big-mouth.'

# 8

I peer into the darkness of a photograph taken eleven years later. In it I am covered in bruises, locked in the study of Vicente's apartment. He has beaten me up as his way of encouraging me to reconsider my behaviour. He insists that a relationship exists between two people and so it's impossible to end one unilaterally. He says he thought I was more intelligent than I actually am.

My back hurts. He twisted my right arm to force me to my knees and bring tears of surrender to my eyes. Then came a couple of blows from his fist and I passed out. Santiago is furious. He races as if electrified along all the routes of my brain. He had made no allowances for violence in his Plan.

'Red alert! This individual is a serious threat to us. Did you hear him say he would put a bullet into us?' I don't answer. I am hurting. I feel humiliated, degraded, in the deepest part of myself.

'The idiot! You just end a romance and it's over. Doesn't he realize this isn't a marriage? It's just an experiment that has run its course.'

'Stop jumping around!' I beg him. 'You're giving me a migraine.'

'The fool! Who does he think he is? We've got to work out a plan right away. Get up!'

'I can't.'

'We've got to get out of here. We need to find a phone and talk to Luis, Javier, Alejandro and Enrique. To all your brothers. It's a family emergency. He's trying to kill us.'

I smile dispiritedly at the inevitable photo. In it, my father, crushed by old age and disgust at life, sits at a chessboard and plays through the openings that made Capablanca a celebrity. It is six in the evening. I see my tall body pass beside him. I pick up a glass and open the fridge to get a drink of chilled water. My father glances at me, then returns to the board and plays Capablanca's next move.

'How did it go?' he asks me, without taking his eyes off the book.

'Fine.' I hear the echo of my voice inside the glass between my mouth and the cold water.

'You look really down these days. Anything happen?'

The water I've just drunk seems to force its way out of my eyes. I rain tears and snot. I confess my love for my classmate Guillermo. I add that Guillermo does not love me.

'What's that?' My father raises his stomach to facilitate a shout. 'Call out the Macho Brigade!'

Three of my brothers appear in the kitchen.

'I want you to beat up this kid who doesn't love my daughter.'

'Why would he love her?' answers Javier. 'Look at her hair.'

'She doesn't wash,' sneers Enrique.

'She never tidies herself up, Dad,' adds Alejandro in his nasal tones.

'And she walks like a dyke,' Enrique says, as the crowning insult.

The photo dissolves in a cackling noise from my father, followed by a chorus of laughter from my brothers.

I am at the end of my tether, and I collapse on the carpet of the study. I hear Santiago's voice in the far distance. In a blue-toned dream I am climbing a stony peak. I scramble to the top and scan the valley below. On the far side of a ravine, on top of a crag of her own, I spy Mina. I want to descend to the foot of the mountain, cross the ravine and reach her. But the valley is suddenly flooded by the sea. Raging waters pound against my rocky peak and hers. Then phosphorescent foam traces on the water symbols, faces, routes to Mina that she illuminates with her moonlike eyes. I speak, but my voice is lost inside the spiral of my ear.

A pounding at the door rouses me. Vicente is back. He rattles his key-chain and through the door asks me menacingly if I've thought things over. Santiago answers him. Vicente opens the door. He picks my body off the floor. He starts to kiss my neck.

'Don't you ever provoke me again,' he says into my ear. 'I don't want to hurt you, understand? Look what I bought you.' He shows me a pair of panties and a bra decorated with red sequins. 'I want you to dance for me.'

'Not today,' I beg.

'I want you to dance like you did at Pedro's party. When you feel like playing the whore, you're going to do it just for me, got it?'

He grabs my chin and hurts me. This is not the old Vicente. His eyes are wild. His soft voice has been replaced by a solemn echo that comes up from the caverns of his stomach.

Santiago controls every word I say. 'Please! You're hurting me. I ache all over. Let me rest. I'll dance for you tomorrow.'

A slide: my first dance in public since the fiasco with Miss Cuquita. To overcome the complexes of childhood is a fundamental part of the Plan. From the time Santiago invaded my body I have practised belly-dancing. By myself, in front of the mirror I have jiggled my stomach in time to a variety of tunes and rhythms. I had not done it in front of anyone else until that day at Pedro's party.

Vicente lets go of me. Behind my back, he says, 'You're not leaving me. You and I were meant for each other.'

# 9

'Yes, I know that,' says Santiago. 'Here's the photo. But we all say things sometimes without thinking.'

Vicente and I had gone out a few times. We used to meet at the Wormwood Café and set out from there to places where we could get to know each other better. Previously, he had invited me back to his apartment, but I refused. This time it was me, spurred on by candle-light and Italian wine, who suggested we go to a motel. Neutral territory was Santiago's thinking. Vicente agreed, somewhat hesitantly. He worried about the hygiene in such places. And somebody from his work might recognize his car. Besides, only women out for one-night stands frequented motels. Better if we went to his apartment. But Santiago insisted, while my breath, calculatedly uncertain, played around Vicente's neck.

We arrive at the motel. We enter, car and all. It is obvious from the photo that this relationship is doomed to failure. Passionate, ardent, with a streak of brutality, Vicente shows off his physical endowments to himself. He forgets about me. He is totally wrapped up in himself, checking out his body in the mirrors. He hasn't the least interest in examining my curves and complexities. Maybe he thinks his massive dick is all any lover's body needs. When he ejaculates, he jerks his body and hurts my neck.

'Did you like it?'

Santiago and I have differing opinions. I want to say that maybe next time we should show a better understanding of each other's needs, but Santiago replies yes, arguing that, with a man like Vicente, it's either say yes or lose him.

I get up and grope uncertainly for a cigarette. Vicente follows me. He stubs out my cigarette and starts his sexual torture. He never gets tired. He can ejaculate as often as he wants. I've only to brush against his arm for him to up-end me and on the floor, sofa, bed or tabletop pull down my panties. Vaseline becomes a primary requirement.

That yes from Santiago, like so many other replies given to Vicente in the course of our relationship, was the prelude to an uncontrollable avalanche of demands. 'If we want to stay with him you'd better learn from his seductive intellect, better experience life as a couple, better give, receive, cook and argue.' Everything my father and brothers challenged me to do by their scornful laughter. If I had practised a difficult honesty, I might still be with Vicente. But there was something else behind Santiago's appeasing dialogues, barricades he erected, as if he were handling a war situation, perhaps out of fear of unleashing a deluge of horrors: abandonment, loss, rejection, helplessness, nakedness and solitude. And behind them yawned the void, an emptiness that the late-night throbbings of my insomnia barely touched on.

I felt like an impostor, especially when Vicente made comments like the one in the last transparency. I am cooking. I am wearing an apron and chopping vegetables for the salad. It is winter. The tomato sauce that is coming to the boil has a sprinkling of oregano on top. Vicente hugs me from behind.

'Pedro says I was real lucky to find a girl like you. Kind. Intelligent. Generous. Most of all, genuine.'

Right. Genuine was the keynote of the public persona Santiago fabricated for me, and I'm getting sick of it.

The void. I got to know it during my childhood, when I was seeking in vain for Mina. I am out in the darkness of the back patio after having been chastized. I can't recall the reason for such a severe punishment, only my father's anger and his carrying me under his arm out to the patio. I hear him threatening the rest of the family. He wags an accusing finger at my cowed mother. Watch out anybody who lets me back inside or brings me a glass of milk for my supper.

Santiago pulls out another photo. He isn't sure if it was taken on the same day. But it might explain my father's rage. I take all the biscuits from the pantry. I grind them under my school shoes. I spread the crumbs like a carpet over the kitchen floor. I like the feel of walking on a crunchy surface. I trace pictures in it as if it were sand. Flour! I take that out as well and mix it with the biscuit crumbs. I add water and create three-dimensional figures.

Santiago hates the bare-faced way I reveal the limits of his power by driving myself closer to the void, but I have learned to still his voice at such times. I even manage to leave him to himself, muttering his complaints endlessly, like a leak drip-dripping into a grotto. He loses something of himself when he does that. When he comes back he is drowsy and has a struggle recognizing things and giving them their right names.

I ought to stop behaving the way I do, he says. He slinks off into a dark, damp cell. His memory goes numb there. His transparencies and photos get a foggy blur on them. People's identities get confused.

Still, for me, isolating him is a survival technique.

The patio is full of rubble. A single mango tree grows in the middle. From it dangles a tomato crate. Higher up, several planks form a sort of floor. It is the tree-house. I have never before been out in the patio in the dark, sentenced to spend the night there. Tonight there is no moon. I am clinging to the house wall, close to the only light that emerges from the kitchen window. At the far end of the patio is stretched a washing-line with bed-sheets drying on it. Near the fence grow a few shrivelled sugar-canes.

All my siblings have spent nights out on the patio. I remember the distress of finding myself in bed, ready to fall asleep, and listening to one of them, the one whose turn it was to be punished, sobbing at my parents' bedroom window and begging to be allowed back inside.

Terror seizes me. The tomato crate, which during the day serves as an elevator up to the tree-house, is now a small coffin squeaking in the breeze. The canes are naked ghosts, desperate to wrap themselves in the bed-sheets. I am alone. Fear pulses in my temples and resonates in my veins.

My mind seeks refuge in my handwriting exercises, my teacher, my school, my mother's smile. With expert skill, the shadows penetrate and annul these memories. I escape to some pleasant transparencies, but they quickly slide away into the canes, into the sheets suspended on the washing-line, into the creaking little coffin. I call out. My voice is lost in the clatter of dishes and the chatter of my family inside the kitchen.

Abruptly, without knowing exactly how, I blot out all my memories. My emptied-out eyes look behind me as I swim underwater in my interior caves. Then comes the void. No memories, no objects there. Nothing. I have returned to the blue abyss and I fall into it. I float there, bodiless, eyeless, without language.

It is a flight into pounding silence. I integrate myself perfectly into the void. Santiago with his image-forming camera is not invited here, so there is no way for him to tell a story about it.

'I'm here, lost in undecipherable space,' I call out to nobody.

Santiago is a creature of the three basic colours and the

twenty-six letters of the alphabet. What is the colour of fear? There is no answer to that in the universe of the spectrum. The hour at which clouds of a colour alien to life pervade us is never registered.

Vicente is furious. He cannot track me down when my eyes turn towards the abyss. 'What happened? Tell me where it all went wrong!'

I am lying recumbent on the sofa. I raise my shoulders, but my glance reveals nothing. We spend days that way. He makes love to me, but I soar away, distant from all feeling. But I can't shake Santiago off this time. He composes phrases, supplies letters of the alphabet, frames a response.

'I don't know what you're talking about,' I say, quoting Santiago.

Vicente jumps up abruptly. 'Forgive me for hitting you.'

'We don't hold grudges,' Santiago whispers in my ear. 'We forgive him everything. The matter is over, purely and simply. We have to get on with our life.'

'It's over and done with.' Again I echo Santiago. Vicente swings around, like a cat pivoting on top of a wall.

'You provoked me. Now you're playing the innocent. What would you have done in my place?'

'Me?' I answer, rising from the blue abyss. 'I would have respected your decision to leave.'

'Me leave? Where would I go?'

# 11

I am travelling by train across Europe. Vicente appears in a distant photo that is crammed with rage. That day had more to it than I've said. He agreed to let me go. While I was packing my suitcase I was planning what I'd say to my mother.

'You were right. You and Lilia were both right.'

With a triumphant smile my mother welcomes me back home. I unpack in the same old untidy bedroom. I hang up my clothes in the wardrobe.

The memory of Vicente tears at me. He begs, like a starving child, for one last night of love. I refuse. I do so because I should have done so in the beginning. The way he keeps on insisting drives me to tell him that sex with him was torture. He saves up his bitterness for the right moment.

'So you never felt anything,' he says, as I head for the door.

I nod my head affirmatively. 'Exactly.'

If Santiago is right about anything, it's that I've no idea how to manage the world of egos and words. When he hears my reply he buries himself in one of his many grottoes. Why do I never find the right thing to say?

Vicente jumps me and tries to pull off my clothes. I push him away. He tries again, and I grab a lamp to smash against his head. He blocks my blow with his forearm. With the flats of my hands I slap out at him. Some slaps hit him full on, others just graze him. He lowers his head and jams it against my stomach. Then he lifts me up and hurls me like a sack on to the bed. Between moans, howls and yells of pain, he manages to tie my hands with a stocking. He spends a few minutes delivering kicks to my body before he succeeds in holding me down and fastening my legs with the sleeves of his shirt.

So there I am. Stretched on the bed, bound hand and foot. Vicente's eyes are wild and his lips are a bright purple. He removes his trousers.

'Control yourself,' the cowardly voice of Santiago tells me, but I have gone far beyond his control and reached the centre of my being. I rip away the veil that masks my anger. I feel a discharge of sulphur that races down my spinal column and crackles in the end of every nerve. Vicente and I are breathing hard in each other's faces. There is something terrified in his stare. His pupils dilate. His eyes scrunch up and release a warm tear. He sits on the edge of the bed, and he covers his face with his hands. He speaks to me. He says things I don't register because Santiago the photographer is reeling from the toxic vapours I've released.

Vicente lets me go.

I leave, full of cramps, with sulphurous saliva still in my mouth. My mind is searching through its maps to find where to close the fissure that still has me retching with its poisons. In the taxi I collect the spattered venom from different parts of my body, pile it into a heap and force it into my protesting stomach. I reach home, doubled with pain. My mother hugs me. It takes me days to get out of bed. I visit the doctor and he prescribes antacids and sleeping pills. Two of my back teeth have come loose for no obvious reason and rock back and forth at the touch of my tongue.

'Never again.' Santiago makes me sign a pact.

'Never,' I promise, enchanted by landscapes of the French countryside I have been perusing lately.

# 12

Of the trip to Europe there exist only a few smudged photos. My tearing the veil that covered my anger condemned me to oscillate between a vague abstractedness and rare moments of specific lucidity.

I had little money with me. After my escape from Vicente, I quit my jobs as a translator and as an engineer – I'd never figured out what I was doing in engineering anyway. I sold my car and a jewelled bracelet that Vicente had bought me when we first started going out. Even so, I had little enough to survive on, just sufficient to travel if I stayed in youth hostels. All the castles, rivers, bridges and museums remained in Santiago's hands like so many old postcards. I was hardly aware of my body as it crossed latitudes and longitudes. I might just as well have been seated in a chair in front of a window, flipping through a book with photos of Europe.

Except, of course, for a few episodes that a puff of memory can blow into holographic life.

In Madrid I stayed at the San Lorenzo lodging-house. It was an ancient building, with four floors and sweeping staircases. The third and fourth floors offered accommodation to single young ladies. On the first floor lived a family; on the second Maria de las Angustias, a woman of around forty, the owner of the building.

When I paid my first month's rent I was hoping to get a job and move on soon to better accommodation. I had no idea I would be stuck there for two whole years.

They assigned me a bed in a room with seven other women. They gave me a key to my wardrobe, along with advice on how to avoid being robbed, instructions on how to light the gas and the rules for keeping the bathroom and the kitchen clean.

In less than an hour after my arrival a blonde Spanish woman adopted me. In her younger days she must have been a beauty. She took me to the market. She introduced me to grocers who wouldn't put their thumbs on the scale when they weighed out fruit and sausage. She suggested stuff to eat, to wash my clothes with, a coffee pot, a frying-pan, wine sold in cardboard containers. With the velocity of a machine-gun she filled me in on who was who among the forty inhabitants of the two floors that made up the lodging-house: the names, the characteristics of thieves, tarts, domestic servants, hairdressers, clerks and women getting government payouts after being declared redundant.

I lay on my bed, my only private space in the room. I was planning how to regulate my finances. I had got it into my head that I would circle the globe. On leaving Mexico, I had crossed the Atlantic, so I had to return via the Pacific. In my diary was a diminutive map of the world, the entire planet spread over two tiny pages.

I marked three key points on it. I would work my way through those places. The first was Spain, the second somewhere in the Middle East, the third Japan. Easy enough to say.

Santiago was happy. Stretching out his silver cord almost to breaking point, he would soar away from me, up into the stratosphere with his camera. From there he would swoop down on particular targets. He was photographing wars, carnival floats with allegorical dragons, the British parliament buildings, political accords. Sometimes he would press through the tunnels of nostalgia and come back with satellite photos of my mother in her kitchen, wrapped in her crocheted woollen blanket, lighting the stove at daybreak.

And so winter arrived. I felt few emotions. I plagiarized my feelings from newspaper photos or from guesses made from outer space. I lay on my bed and stayed there. I got up only twice a day, once to give an English class in the morning, once to give two classes in the evening. This brought in enough for me to pay for my lodging, to eat badly and to buy unmarked, home-made red wine by the gallon through a government pensioner named Lola.

I didn't feel lonely. Santiago kept himself so busy filling his album with shots from all over the world that he hardly muttered his fears. Time and again, as I lay in bed listening to the other women snoring, he would come stumbling out of his caves with a photo in his hand, to ask me where was this or that person who had featured at some point in the movie of our life. So many questions that they gave my heart palpitations. His nagging would drive me out of bed to grope for the container of wine. A cigarette, a lamp and a book were the best sedative. We would entertain ourselves with photos of writers – Spanish, French or English – until we fell asleep. Sometimes we went to see a movie, but we always came out with our head spinning. We would kill time trying to match the intermittent way our memory worked with the efficient way the memories of the characters operated.

Months of peace drifted by before the next photo in the album, one that Santiago points to with embarrassment. It is the final days of winter. Already the people of Madrid are strolling the streets in light jackets. Santa Barbara Square is thronging with young men drinking their first cold beer and a few old boys sipping red wine. I come up out of the mouth of the Metro.

I am heading back to my lodgings. I don't know exactly why, but Santiago forces me to stop suddenly half-way across the square. Loaded with his bagfuls of photographs of other people, of strangers with their peculiar odours and foreign ways under an alien moon, he says to me in a tone I have learned to fear, 'This is no good.'

Just like that, giving no reasons. He hurls at me the bags of photos, and they create a knot in the nape of my neck. I am still living with one foot over the edge of the abyss, not fully part of the concrete world, a happy position for anyone who has always seen herself as a stranger to life. Hypothetically, without registering objects named by human eyes, I try to move forwards.

'We'll talk about it later in bed,' I tell him.

'No. No. And no again.'

Santiago is determined to harass me. He drums out questions in my encephalic arteries. Where is she now, the absent woman who loves us so? Where is the grave of the cruel old man? Where is Lilia, dancing for joy? Where today, exactly where today, in what part of the garden back home, is the Macho Brigade celebrating the arrival of the weekend?

'We carry them all inside us,' he hears me say without conviction. The English texts fall from my hands. The people near by scurry away, anxious not to be involved in an embarrassing scene. Everything turns into a silent movie. Beating on his drum and weeping, Santiago begs to be allowed to recognize at least one person in the crowd around us. I tremble uncontrollably. I want to pick up my books, but I manage to do it only in my imagination.

I plead with him. 'Don't do this to me in the middle of the square!'

Square? What square? There is no square, only an unrecognizable darkness, a sort of grey but not grey, for grey would be a colour that would let me act.

I don't know how long I was stranded there, but I felt as empty as I did during my suicide attempt, before Santiago arrived. What did I do? I have no idea. How did I get back to my lodgings with my books under my arm and get into the bed that protected me from all things alien? I have no idea.

# 13

I was recovering from the moment in the square when I glanced in the direction of the dormitory windows. Santiago was nowhere to be seen. Most likely he was dangling from some precipice, trying not to fall. Adriana, a handsome, middle-aged Galician woman with a fair complexion, was standing in front of the windows. She was combing out her long dark hair. Without Santiago's presence the windows could mean only a vertigo similar to the one you experience when you position yourself between two facing mirrors. They trick you. At first they provide you with new vistas, but then they trap you in an endlessly dizzying panorama of images.

The windows, which belonged to the eight women who slept there, overlooked a central patio, with a disused fountain crowned by the statue of a naked child. By day it was filled by birds; at night by tom-cats on the prowl. By now it was already dark, and I could sense the stealthy approach of the cats.

Stretched out on my bed, I tried again and again to explain to the abyss the reasons behind my trip. Suddenly I jumped up and grabbed Adriana by her long hair. With tears in my eyes I begged her to get away from the windows. Couldn't she see the danger she was in, visible from all sides, reflected in the windows?

'Look,' I told her, 'we're all able to see you there. Just look!' I tugged hard on her hair.

Adriana did what I had done in the photo of Felicitas. She clutched the roots of her hair to lessen the pain.

I managed to drag her to the floor.

At that point I would have gone quietly back to bed, but Maria de las Angustias intervened. She took me down to the second floor.

'Tea or coffee?' she asked.

'Nothing,' I replied.

'Sweetheart,' she said in English. She'd have loved to speak entirely in English if she'd known how. How appropriate for a woman of Moorish blood! 'You know I just adore you. I've never allowed anyone to get three months behind with the rent before. You are the sole exception.' Her words had a hollow ring to them, like a lecture from the boss. 'But you've gone way too far!'

Where are you, Santiago? Now that I need to find a reply! The weather is still cold, so you can't be sleeping yet in railway stations or places like that.

'She was standing by the window,' I replied as my only possible defence.

'Adriana has spent nine years here looking out of the windows.'

'Somebody had to tell her.'

'For some inexplicable reason, I really like you, dear, but there is no way I can allow you to bother another lodger. Are we agreed on that? Good. What would you say to a liqueur or a glass of wine?'

'I don't want anything,' I replied as before.

Maria de las Angustias came closer. The smell emanating from her breasts was like my mother's.

'If you bother anybody again you'll force me to throw you out. Understand?'

Without further ado she accompanied me up the stairs back to the lodging area of which she was queen. There she spoke to Vicenta, the woman in charge of the fourth floor. Without asking my opinion, they entered a tiny room beside the kitchen and, between them, dragged out of it old scrap metal, a disused toilet bowl and black rubbish bags filled with something or other. Then they hauled my bed and wardrobe in there.

'This place will suit you better. You'll have more privacy here.'

I flopped down on the bed. The room was barely big enough to

44

accommodate the bed, the wardrobe and a coffee-table. It had no windows and the door opened directly on to the kitchen. It was one of the many unused storage cupboards in the building. It had all the characteristics of a coffin.

## 14

Sitting on the edge of the bed Santiago and I pulled out photos that left us brimful of nostalgia before we fell asleep, body and soul. The first one we looked at left me staring up at the ceiling of my closet-room. It showed the death of my father. After all he had suffered it had come as a relief both to him and to us. Of course nobody with his level of vanity could die a straightforward death. He had to sidle into it, surreptitiously, sinking into a coma after an operation for appendicitis that had serious complications. For the two weeks he was in the coma, he wore an expression of pain. Tears rolled down from his shut eyes whenever we spoke to him. According to the doctor, chatting to a patient increases that person's will to live and to rouse himself from his comatose state. My siblings and I surrounded his bed at all times. By this time I was in secondary school. I made up stories about my teachers that I knew would amuse him. In my father's judgement, every teacher in the world was an idiot, apart from the Buddha, Jesus, Mohammed, Confucius and my father himself. All of humanity had produced only two engineers worth their salt: Albert Einstein and himself.

I can still see his face, toughened and creased, the enormous beer belly, the skinny legs. He is curled up in the foetal position, apparently unconscious. That is how we left him, Santiago and I, when we passed on to other photos.

Then I get off the bed and stand up. In my wardrobe are big bottles of wine and plastic cups. As I uncork a bottle and pour out a drink it occurs to me that I should apologize to Adriana.

In a moment or two I'll take her a glass of wine and we'll raise a toast together in honour of her forgiving me.

Santiago grumbles at the idea. 'Get some sense!' he tells me. 'That woman is as shallow as they come. She's not worth the trouble.'

'You sound exactly like my dad,' I smile. 'Say what you like, I'm going to ask her to forgive me.'

'What you should do is apologize to Maria de las Angustias. God! Where the hell did she get a name like that?'

After stifling his laughter Santiago reels off the benefits she has given us: our own room, her open affection, her fondness for my personality, especially for my look of an orphan in a strange land.

'You call this a room?' I snort. 'It's a storage cupboard, and I know she stuck me in here to punish me. Look at those stairs. God knows where they lead.'

Santiago gives a nervous jump.

'Look at them. Over there.' I am determined to rattle him.

I step out of my 'private room'. The kitchen reeks of the lingering cooking smells of the government pensioners' supper. And it's already way past 10 p.m.! According to the rules, the kitchen is closed by ten. It still stinks of garlic, fry-ups, sausages and strong coffee. The small door to the little staircase is half-open. I open it fully, and the hinges squeak. Nothing is visible inside. Santiago pulls out his photo of the staircase where the Kid with the Candle stalked.

Was that taken before or after my night on the patio? It had to be after. A house with a patio would have been too expensive for my parents to rent by that date.

After a squabble with his superiors – they were all a bunch of sly, incompetent frauds – my father picked up some work in land-surveying and drafting, but he didn't earn enough to allow us to predict whether we were going to meet our monthly expenses or whether we would be living without electricity or gas and dodging the rent-collector.

My father then lost those two jobs, but that just tripled his vanity. What he didn't lose, for sure, was his sense of humour, as cruel as an adolescent king's.

I have already said that I had gaps in my understanding. In this photo I see myself listening one night to one of my father's innumerable stories. My brothers and my sister are clustered around him. By the look of it we've just moved into a new place. There are cardboard boxes everywhere. My mother opens them and silently arranges plates, fruit bowls and plaster ornaments. My father has gathered us around him to give us some ghastly news: this is the apartment where a little boy died at the very time he was about to make his first communion. Dropped dead! Boom! Here he was, rehearsing his part in the ceremony and then, for no reason, he just fell down dead! And now his ghost haunts this place, carrying a candle in its hand, most often appearing on the stairs leading up to the apartment.

'If any of you see him,' whispers my father, 'there's no need to be scared. All you have to do is recite the "Our Father" three times and zip' – my father snaps his fingers – 'he'll disappear. And if he doesn't, just keep on praying.'

Pray? Appear? Disappear? 'Our Father'? I don't get it. I stare at the horrified faces of my teenage siblings. Dear, all-knowing Lilia, do you know the 'Our Father'? If you do, I'll soap your back for a whole week when we take a bath together. I won't steal your crayons ever again. And I'll scratch your back in bed as well!

'Well now,' says my father with a gravity that would fool any-body. 'Let's put that aside and you, Javier,' he addresses my brother, the one with the little hand that comes and goes, 'I want you to slip down to the store and get me some beer.'

My brother cringes visibly. Leaving the apartment means going down the spooky staircase, which has no electric light. The light sockets in its majestic walls are so high that when a light bulb fuses it stays fused. Daylight reveals that the heights are thick with cobwebs. My brother begs for mercy and bursts into tears.

'Don't be soft!' my father yells at him. 'That's all I need, a queer in the family. Get moving, you cry-baby!'

My father gives a superb imitation of righteous rage before

48

sneaking off to chuckle behind our backs. But it is only years later that I twig this. Right now he has his eyebrows arched, a stare like a dagger and his lips narrowed, squeezed tight under this thick, ponderous moustache.

Javier steps out of the ring we had formed around my father. 'If I meet the Kid with the Candle,' Javier babbles hopelessly, 'I know I'll die.' Then he holds out his hand for the money my father is pulling from his pocket and disappears, his knees quaking, out of the door that leads to the stairs.

Who could I turn to in this moment of desperation? To Mina? Floating in mid air, a sketchy outline at best by night and day, shaded in only by the smile of the twilight? Mina who had nothing to do with the objective world? Mina who responded intuitively to my body, my adrenaline and my blood when it boiled? Mina as blue as outer space? Mina the laughing one? Eyeless Mina who still knew where to tread? Mina disconcerted by the complexities of the adult mind? Mina who was all warm embrace and patience? Tell me, will Javier make it back? Mina is unfamiliar with stairs, with light bulbs and candles, but she senses the vibration of my nerves and she breathes a breath of security on to me. Mina offers me peace. But Mina brings no understanding, and, as I lie in bed, I cling to the back of my sister Lilia. I start to scratch it.

Suddenly screams ring out. My heart misses a beat and then starts to race.

I am sitting on my bed. I want to wake Lilia up but I cannot move. Again the screams. They are not coming from Javier. They belong to the Kid with the Candle. No. No. They are my father's. He calls out, he begs for mercy. He shouts out who he is. Then come the sounds of blows and more screams, this time in a younger voice, from the stairwell. I weep. I call for my mother. No answer. Only absence.

At last I can move. I am wearing flannel pyjamas. I reach the door handle and open the door. I am dying of fear, and Mina tells me, 'Use your eyes and you will see.'

So I open them. I see my father stretched out on the sofa in the living-room. My mother is pressing raw steak to his face. My brother, Javier, still carrying a heavy stick in his hand, stands beside them, his head bowed, sobbing.

The next photo comes from Javier's album. While I was scratching Lilia's back to get her to teach me the secret of the 'Our Father' that would make the Kid with the Candle disappear, Javier had gone down the staircase without incident. He reached the store and asked for the beers for my father. So far, no problem. On his return, while he was climbing the first curve of the winding staircase, he saw a flickering light coming towards him. It was undoubtedly a candle, the flame on its wick trembling in the night air. Armed with a branch he had found lying in the garden, he bided his time until the Kid with the Candle came within striking distance. It was too late when he realized that he had clubbed his own father, wrapped in a sheet and carrying a candle.

I used a cigarette lighter to illuminate the spooky staircase in the San Lorenzo lodging-house. With a courage supplied by my memory of Javier, I went down the narrow stairs that had scarcely room for my size-four shoes. There were fifteen stairs at most. I found myself in front of another small door, just like the one above. I tried to open it, but it was locked. I assumed it opened on to the kitchen on the third floor. Maybe there was somebody on the other side of the door right now, wondering where it led. If I ever made a friend on the third floor we could use this staircase to see each other in secret.

But that day never arrived. It isn't easy to make friends when you're beset by a Santiago fanatically concerned with mental health. He begs me not to get involved with others. But we've always been sociable, I tell him. Right! The way you were with poor Martha in primary school!

'That was before you came into my life.'

'And your pal in the Faculty of Engineering?'

It's obvious that Santiago and I have different ideas about friendship. After a whole year here in Spain I am still solitary. That night, after discovering that the stairs led only to a locked door, I went back up to my closet-room to get my wine. I poured out two drinks in plastic cups. I crept through the darkness of the lodging-house where I'd slept, only a few hours before, next to the seven other women. I waited for my eyes to adjust to the darkness before I could pick up Adriana's bed. I went up to her with the wine in my hands. 'Adriana?' I whispered.

No reply.

'Adriana!' I insisted.

Immediately screams pierced the night air, as puzzling to me as those from the stairs haunted by the Kid with the Candle. Adriana was peering at me through the gloom and screaming in panic. To her way of thinking she was being menaced by a satanic shadow. I decided to race back to my closet-room, but it was too late. Several of the other women had switched on their bedside lamps.

Every single one of them testified against me in front of Maria de las Angustias. They swore I'd tried to attack Adriana in the dark of the night. According to them, I had scissors in one hand and in the other something they could not identify, but, without a doubt, it was a sharp pointed object.

I found myself once again confronted by the gypsy-dark eyes of the owner of the lodging-house. Utterly convinced that I would establish my innocence, I showed her the two cups of wine. I explained things to her while Santiago darted around my brain hysterically, yelling, 'I told you so, I told you so!' I had only come to make peace, I pleaded. I'd come to ask forgiveness.

'At a quarter to one in the morning?'

What did the time matter? If we all were to ask pardon for our errors the world would be free of hatred, and what would the time of day matter?

'Look, Maria, we think differently in the night, not the same as in the day. The moon has a powerful influence on us. Yes, it's weighed down with old bitternesses, and that's why it's sterile. Everybody knows that. But, all the same, its light brushes against us gently. The sun, on the other hand, overloads us with information. We do our best to understand it, but the bloody thing just dazzles us. But the moon, the night, the stars, they're the best time to be truly humane, especially when it's a matter of making discoveries about God and the universe, the dimensions and all that sort of stuff. That's why they get out their telescopes at night.'

'This wine or the other?' I finally managed to say, when she and I got back to my room.

'This one,' she answered distantly, as if she were winding up for a sermon.

'I'm sorry you have to sit on my bed, but there's no space here for a chair.'

'So you're not happy with your room?'

'No, no, Maria. It's a fine room. I just love it. By the way, did you ever notice those stairs over there?'

'Yes. They lead down to the third floor.'

'Is that all? I was imagining a load of secret passages . . .'

She didn't let me finish. Between sips of wine she jotted down a number on the back of a business card and said in a horribly maternal tone, 'This is the best I can do for you.' She passed me the card. It was the phone number of a psychiatrist. 'You've been here for over a year. You hardly ever go out. You don't talk to anybody. You drink far too much. I wouldn't know who to call if you had an accident. Vicenta tells me that somebody called Cuco calls you almost every day. He's some relative, she says.'

## 15

Refugio 'Cuco' Vidal. I had told Vicenta, the only person author-
ized to answer the phone, to say to anyone asking for me that I had
died, left town, been declared insane or anything else she liked. So
Vicenta wouldn't have talked to him. She had merely assumed he
was a relative.

I had met Refugio in a bar, the Double Diamond, one Satur-
day night.

My bones were aching from lying in bed so much. Santiago
had been bashing holes in my brain, skidding around on tobog-
gans of blood.

'What are we doing here?' he had wanted to know. 'We don't
belong in a dump like this.'

'You didn't say that when Maria put me there. You said it was a
lovely place.'

'I don't mean your bedroom. I mean this whole crappy lodging-house.'

He stabbed me with something sharp on my head, and I felt a
searing pain.

'You see? It hurts, doesn't it? You're developing a hole in your
head. What's worse is it isn't marked on my maps. I get dizzy just
peering into it. I've lost a lot of photos and plans down there. Now
I'm sure we'll never make it to Japan. Five letters, T-o-k-y-o, just
fell into it.'

'We can't go anywhere. We have no money. We're not even in
good physical shape. We've no energy, no enthusiasm.'

'Oh, it's enthusiasm you want, is it? No problem. I just press a
button here and your life picks up speed. See?'

He made me jump out of bed and cross over to the mirror.

How long had it been since I'd taken a good look at myself? I'd put on six or seven pounds, my skin was yellower than ever and I had deep bags under my eyes, violet-tinted around the edges and greenish in the grooves. My mouth was turned down. My lips had lost the cute little mounds that Vicente had loved to nibble. I had lost several molars recently. My tongue was striped with bands of yellow and white. My hair, however, had retained its abundance and its lustre. My eyes, too, were still the same, although I had to squeeze them hard to get them to focus on my reflection in the mirror. Santiago kept yacking on about the dangers of the void I had unearthed.

'I've a feeling something's slipping away,' he complained.

'As long as it's only those sacks of photos you chucked out in the square.'

'No. It's something far worse. There's some saliva that's starting to dribble out. It stings me. It makes me flinch. It sidelines me.'

I scrambled around in my mind for some photo I could use to compare situations. Meanwhile I was changing my clothes. I dabbed on deodorant and a lemony lotion. I combed my hair. I outlined my eyes with eye-shadow and pinched my lips to bring back some of their pouting fullness.

'I'm telling you this hole is not on my maps. And I know it's all because of your lifestyle.' He then added in a sing-song, infantile voice, 'From work to bed, from bed to kitchen, from kitchen to bed, from bed to wardrobe to get your booze, from booze to bed, from bed to work, from work . . .'

I ignored him. I went through several changes of clothes before I was satisfied with my appearance. Once again I looked like a 23-year-old woman, poured into my tight jeans, with a navy-blue blouse. My chestnut hair hung half-way down my back.

Santiago continued his whine. 'I just know you're going to do something stupid. That stinging saliva is rising again. You're in real danger of going to a bar. That's where we're heading, isn't it?

That's where you're going to lose control. Then we'll be coming back with gaps in our memory, black holes, after trips to God-knows-where. Haven't I told you before what your dreams are like when you drink too much?'

He then played one of his old tricks, and hundreds of images came tumbling down like hammers hitting glass. He managed to make me dizzy just at the moment I was going down the steps outside the building.

But a few minutes later I was opening the door of the Double Diamond bar. Blaring music, shrieking laughter and strong drink. I took a seat at the bar and ordered a beer for starters. I observed the crowd. The bartender told me a couple of jokes, and I pretended to laugh at them. I was in the middle of laughing when Refugio – 'Cuco' – Vidal appeared. He had come over to pick up drinks for his friends who were seated at a small, round table.

Cuco was a pint-sized Spaniard, dark-skinned and excessively thin. He smoked non-stop and had a permanent wheeze. He must have been around forty. He asked me if I was alone. I told him I was waiting for a friend. It wasn't a total lie. Sometimes women from the third floor, who for some reason were generally younger than those on the fourth, used to gather in this bar and invite me to join their chattering group. I used to pull up a chair, but I never contributed more than the occasional smile. So it wasn't beyond possibility that they could show up at any moment.

I didn't keep count of the beers I drank. Cuco reappeared at my side and pointed out that my friend hadn't arrived.

'You're very pretty, you know,' he said.

Despite the drunkenness and all, Santiago always had a considered riposte in his armoury for just such chat-up lines. But I was thinking how terrible I had looked in the mirror of the lodging-house.

'Really?' I said. 'You should have seen me a couple of hours ago.'

Santiago protested that this was not one of our well-rehearsed responses.

'But anyway,' I added quickly, 'thanks for the compliment.'

Santiago managed a sigh of approval.

'Can I buy you a drink?'

'A beer.'

By now Cuco had noticed that my accent was not Spanish.

'You're not from around here, are you?'

'No.'

'You don't like to say much, do you?'

I took a swig of the beer and looked at him closely. The only attractive thing about him was the far-away look in his sad eyes.

'No, but I do like to have sex.'

Santiago hit the roof of one of his caves, exploding with fury. This remark defied every plan of his, lacked any vestige of his treasured elegance. I drank some more of the beer and drowned his rage in it.

Cuco paid my bill, said goodbye to his friends and led me outside, slipping his arm around my waist.

His car smelt new. I told him I was hungry. Cuco drove away slowly, as if we were long-time lovers without any haste. He took me to a stylish restaurant where the waiters knew him by name.

Since my time with Vicente, I had not eaten in a place with such a splendid menu. I ordered a glass of red wine, cream of artichoke soup, a spinach salad and a New York steak. Cuco gave me a tender look. He ordered only the artichoke soup.

We were eating the soup when he started to vomit. He had the delicacy to mask his mouth with his napkin and managed to vomit into the plate without attracting the waiters' attention. He made hardly any noise. He just jerked back and forth and gave a few soft moans. My reaction was to feel an urge to vomit, too, out of disgust. I jumped up from the table and dashed to the bathroom.

Santiago grabbed me there. 'Revolting! Ugh! How can anyone

vomit soup into soup? It isn't enough for this bloke to be ugly, but he has to vomit over his food? We're really slumming it here tonight and no mistake!'

Stay cool, I told myself, while I retched up two spoonfuls of soup and lots of beers. Vomiting the excess of alcohol led directly to the emergence of Santiago at his most lucid.

'Let's go home,' he said.

I gathered all my forces against him. I was thinking about that New York steak.

'Just listen to his cough. He's going to infect us. He's got something seriously wrong with him. One look at him tells you he's a walking plague.'

I left the bathroom. Cuco was smoking and drinking. A noble-hearted waiter had removed the plate with the vomit. The spinach and the meat arrived. Cuco gave me more tender looks.

'Carry on,' he said.

But I could not. As soon as I cut into the steak Santiago rose up in protest, and the thought of Cuco's spasms and the soup plate brimming with vomit overcame my drunken will to indulge myself.

'Wine. I'd like more wine, please.'

A bottle of the best Rioja arrived at the table.

We chatted. It turned out he was another engineer. He was from Catalonia and was building a new line of the Madrid Metro. While Santiago swung back and forth between mortal fear and blistering rage, I told Cuco I was from Colombia. I was studying for a master's degree in literature. We talked about various authors. We kept on drinking; he hardly anything, I lots.

We left the restaurant arm in arm and went back to his place. He started up the jacuzzi. He put on some music, and we danced. We got into the tub of hot water naked. Undressed, he looked like a Jewish prisoner from a concentration camp. His body was stunted and covered in small sores, some of them scabbed over, others bleeding. He smiled all the time.

'Grotesque!' was the comment I got from Santiago. In a surly, disdainful voice he was reciting an endless catalogue of the vilest epithets for my lover all the time I was kissing him. As we headed towards the bed Santiago brandished the photo of the cat.

It is the year before my suicide attempt, and I am sitting at home in a battered armchair staring into the void. A horrible stink catches my attention. I look around to see where it is coming from. A cat is hiding behind the chair. From the rim of one of its eyes maggots of all sizes are wriggling their way out; from the other tears. It gives me goose-bumps just to look at it, but I do not run away. On the contrary. My only thought is to get it out of the house before my father finds it and batters it with his boots. As I get closer to the cat I see it has another maggoty wound under its chin.

The cat just sits there. Maggots are crawling all over its body and then back into the exposed flesh. I feel a sense of horror, and shivers run up my back. A car has hit the cat at some time. Then somebody has stoned it, and now it is not far from its grave. I want to pick the cat up, but the maggots on its sides stop me.

Finally I pick it up in a kitchen towel and creep with it past the bedroom where my parents are taking an afternoon nap. Out on the patio I put it in a trough. I speak words of consolation to it, but they are really meant to bring comfort to me. I want to end its suffering with a deadly blow, but I cannot bring myself to hit it. I have no poison. Its one healthy eye continues to weep in misery. I tell it to wait, and I go to fetch an aspirin from the medicine cabinet.

I come back with four and dissolve them in warm water. With a dropper I put the liquid in its mouth, and it runs out through the wound in its gullet. Many maggots also drop out. I decide to wash its wounds. With warm water I begin to flush out the maggots, but many of them only flee deeper inside the body. I can do no more. I feel desperate and helpless. I leave the cat wrapped in the kitchen towel in a corner of the patio. Two days later it is dead.

Cuco is on top of me, kissing me. Beside us is a lamp, and by its light I can see the same suffering in his eyes. Blindly I choose a sore on his back and run the pad of my finger over it as if it were an antique Egyptian scarab lately discovered by an anthropologist. Then I choose another and another. They are like the maggots in the cat, only fossilized on his skin. He is embarrassed and hides his face in my neck. After we caress each other for a while he starts to cough. First a few dry heaves, then a crackling burst of phlegm. He wants to get off the bed, but the coughing doubles him over. He manages to hold one hand to his mouth, but blood-streaked phlegm slips out between his fingers. He covers his head with the sheet. Coughing and reeling he heads to the bathroom. From the bed I can hear him spitting and choking. I hear him pull back the sliding door of the medicine cabinet and the clinking of glass bottles. He takes a long swallow of medicine and comes out of the bathroom grinning, ready to carry on with his caresses. Santiago, still in a sulky voice, begs that we get out of there.

'Take me back to the lodging-house,' I say to Cuco.

'No, no!' protests Santiago. 'Don't let him take you there. He ought not to know where you live. Phone for a taxi.'

I have no will left to argue. My head is spinning from so much alcohol, from vomiting and wild emotions. I take the easy way out. Cuco drops me off at the door of the San Lorenzo. He hugs me fiercely. He asks for my phone number. My thoughts are not on the horror of the maggots eating the cat alive but on its death two days later. I give him my number.

## 16

Sunday morning dawned with an acute sense of crisis. As I awoke, I could smell on me the sickly odours of Cuco's kisses and taste fermented wine in the corners of my mouth. Santiago was insisting we swallow a whole box of antibiotics.

'You've got to rinse your teeth with alcohol. Then gargle. Maybe Maria de las Angustias could let us have some antiseptic mouthwash.'

Getting out of bed I discovered thrust under the door a letter from Mexico. It must have arrived on Friday. It bore signs of having been opened and resealed. The sender's name was my mother's. Before I read it I thought for a moment and speculated that Maria de las Angustias, anxious about my health, had opened it, but when I read the contents – as much of them as I could read because my mother had written in felt pen and her tears had smudged many parts of them – I nearly fainted.

Darling little daughter,

[Erased] well, but I am very worried by the [erased] Spain. I know your character and [erased] thirst for justice. I hope you're not involved [erased] of terrorism. If you can't [erased] the Basque terrorist organization, you always have your family. Even if we have to sell [erased] Reverse the charges. All of us here love you. Javier says [erased] school. Probably [erased] Seek political asylum in the Mexican Consulate.

Kisses and [erased] us all.

Your mum, who loves you

'What on earth . . . ?' cried Santiago. 'What's got into your mother?'

'Ssshh! Let me think.'

'Think? There's no time to think. We've got to pack and get out of here fast. They're going to stick us in gaol because they believe you're in league with the Basque terrorists, and once inside we're going to die from the disease Cuco infected us with.'

I reread the letter several times. I checked the envelope. It had certainly been opened. I toyed with the hope that my mother had sealed it, found the glue wasn't holding and then stuck it down more firmly with drops of white paste. But if that were so I would have got the letter on Friday, not on Sunday morning.

Santiago kept imploring me to get us out. We would hang out in a railway station, reverse the charges to Mexico to ask for money and go back home. His belief was that the letter had been opened not in the lodging-house but in the offices of the Spanish counter-terrorism branch. Of course they had already contacted Maria de las Angustias, and she was reporting back to them on our suspicious behaviour.

He managed to put me into a state of panic. I sat on the edge of my bed, my face in my hands. Where did my mother ever get such a wild idea? We began to scour the photograph files in search of an image that suggested I was a potential guerrilla. But, as we flicked through them there was only one that possessed anything like ideological content, and that lacked all traces of insurgent courage. However, there were dozens where, at Santiago's urging, I had lied extravagantly to my family.

While images flashed across the screen in rapid succession, Santiago's alarm caused me terrifying anxieties.

'You can bet for sure that the whole Guardia Civil is outside the door right now.'

I made as if to lie back down on the bed.

'No!' screamed Santiago. 'Pack your stuff. Let's get out of here!'

I pulled some clean clothes out of the wardrobe and put on my sandals to walk to the bathroom. If I could only leave Santiago here in my bedroom, or anywhere, and have a moment to think for myself! Then I inched open the door of my room, scared that I would find myself staring down the muzzle of a sniper's rifle.

In the bathroom I allowed the hot water to cascade over my shoulders. What was to be done? The worst thing would be to take Santiago's advice and make a run for it. That would simply confirm suspicions. For the moment the wisest course of action was to stay put.

The letter hardly seemed typical of my mother. She was never a woman to worry. She wandered through life with a blithe carelessness, always laying what few concerns she had on the shoulders of Divine Providence. The photographic evidence makes that plain.

Here she is walking along, her nose in the air. We are in the town centre. The streets are crammed with people and traffic. My brothers and sisters and I trail behind her. We are out on a trip to buy uniforms and shoes for school. Because of my diminutive size and the masses of people, I keep losing sight of her and my siblings. I have to gallop after them. We reach a junction. My mother looks right, then left and crosses. She forgets that she has a train of children trotting after her. We all try to cross with her. Suddenly a car comes racing towards us.

'Look out!'

We hurtle back to the pavement. Meanwhile my mother is on the far side of the street and carries on walking. Alejandro, the tallest, shades his eyes and tries to pick out her dark, curly hair.

'Everybody grab a hand,' says Javier. 'One, two, three!'

We cross in one long chain. Pulled by Enrique, I almost fly across the junction. When we get to the other side we let go and it's everyone for himself, darting past human obstacles until we reach the shop window where my mother, blissfully indifferent to our problems, is peering at the display of goods.

Santiago pulls up another photo that confirms my mother's detachment from the world around her. This is one of my first memories. It is here that my fear of abandonment is chillingly featured. I am around two years old. We are going on a trip somewhere. We climb aboard a bus and find a seat. While other passengers are boarding, Lilia, instead of sitting down, gets off through the back door. Suddenly Alejandro sees her through the bus window. 'Mum! Lilia got off!'

My mother races to the back door and jumps off the bus. All my brothers follow her and, I am left there. Before the bus speeds away the last thing I see through the window is the six bodies of my family, until that moment the only bodies my infantile antennae can recognize, all grouped cheerily around Lilia. I am terrified, but I do not make a sound. Thanks to my intuition or my terror, I make myself as tiny as I can as I travel alone on the bus.

Santiago smiles at the next image. I am at the police station. A policeman buys me an ice-cream cone. He strokes my hair and tells me not to worry, that my mother is on her way.

There is always some compensation for being abandoned.

## 17

I try to explain everything in a goodbye letter to Reginald. I thank him for his infinite tenderness, for his protection. I tell him that, although I know my leaving will hurt him and my proficiency in English take him by surprise, I had needed him to help me escape from a mystical earthquake, a volcano spouting magma up from the depths of the abyss. That was the condition I saw myself in when I arrived in London at around Christmas time.

Back in Madrid I had found Santiago fenced in, surrendered, terrified, threatened. By then I had realized that he used every occasion when my life felt unsatisfactory to extend his dominion over me. So I was glad I had stayed put rather than run off in a profound depression. Even so I had had to book an appointment with the psychiatrist recommended by Maria de las Angustias.

He was the director of an asylum on the outskirts of Madrid. Thanks to Maria de las Angustias he wasn't going to charge me anything, but I could see him only at ten o'clock at night. 'Every day, if you don't mind.'

My conflict with Santiago had now reached distressing proportions. His paranoia had extended to unsuspected limits. The letter from my mother suggesting that we belonged to a terrorist organization convinced him that I had been entrapped in a plot concocted by Maria, the psychiatrist and the Spanish government. Maria now started to visit me frequently and ask all sorts of questions. Santiago answered her with all sorts of lies.

'When are you going to see José Luis? He really will help you.'

Climbing up the asphalt path, sparsely lit by a few mercury lamps set at ground level, I passed through the steep gardens of the enormous hospital. It was at this point I was tempted to believe Santiago. There would be no way back. I observed the heavily barred windows and the closed shutters. Santiago played his old trick of jumping around my temples in an attempt to prevent me from entering. Once inside we would never be allowed to leave, he alleged. But in the end my curiosity simply won out.

After I had waited a few minutes in the reception area José Luis appeared. With a gesture he invited me to follow him down the passageways. Everything was in silence. The doctor's rubber shoes and my moccasins made no sound on the gleaming floors. We passed down several corridors before we reached his office. He sat in an armchair with a high back and indicated for me to sit on a chair facing his desk. A small lamp on it illuminated only his chest and my face.

'Well then?'

'Don't say a word to him!' ordered Santiago. 'This isn't an asylum. It's just like one of those torture chambers they use in Argentina. It's a secret prison. Get out of here while you can. Tell him you're going to the toilet and make a run for it.'

I started to cry, first out of fear, then out of rage, finally I don't know for what reason. I wept through my nose, my eyes, my mouth. All the doctor did was to reach for disposable handkerchiefs and pass me some. The ball of paper in my hands got bigger and bigger, as if an avalanche from my mouth had produced it. I struggled to stop crying, but I couldn't. I was totally ashamed of my behaviour.

It happened that way at all our interviews. I would arrive at the hospital, wait for him to turn up, and he would come for me, then we would walk in silence down the glistening hallways, we would arrive at his office and I would promptly burst into tears. After a week of this he ignored the clock indicating the end of the session and, tilting the lamp so that it lit up his eyes, said to me, 'You have a mental block.' He interlocked the fingers of both hands. 'My suggestion is that you come here for one more week while you make preparations to go back to Mexico.'

'What about Tokyo?' Santiago protested. 'What about that map of the world we planned our trip on? This doctor is a head-case. We'd be better off not seeing him again. Maybe he isn't a doctor. I bet the real doctor is tied up in the basement.'

After that Santiago produced photos he had faked, images of the rest of the world that we had planned to see. In them I appeared wearing an elegant business suit, smiling obliquely just like my sister Lilia and speaking Japanese in some boardroom or other. Since he had no personal experience of life in those far-away places, he would flash before me startling snapshots in which I was walking in down-at-heel sandals, following in the footsteps of some lama across an oriental desert.

He insisted on displaying fragments from my future. Here I was at carnivals, there at temples. All the same, I thought the doctor had made a good point. I ought to get away from Spain. But to ask my family for money would be an admission of financial incompetence, and I had left Mexico to demonstrate my ability to succeed, to gobble up the world as if it were my personal oyster. It would also put my siblings in the embarrassing position of having to chip in enough money to buy me a ticket home.

Santiago suggested that we speak to Refugio Vidal.

## 18

Once again we are seated in an upmarket restaurant, but this time I wear a face of inconsolable woe. I decline to eat anything, and I adopt the far-away look I learned from my mother. Cuco tilts his head from side to side like a dog unable to understand his master's commands. He smiles at me. Finally the inevitable question arrives: 'What's the matter?'

Abetted by the memory of the psychiatrist's verdict, I start to weep. But with exemplary refinement I collect my tears in the cloth napkin.

'This is daylight robbery!' I hear myself protesting to Santiago, who has holed up in his den trying to avoid the alcohol fumes.

'I have a dreadful problem,' Santiago whines to Cuco. 'My brother Vicente is terribly sick in hospital and I need to get back to Colombia to see him.' I conjure up the image of my ex-lover, his face eroded by cancer, and I wince. 'But I haven't got a penny.'

'How much do you need?'

'Six hundred dollars!' I pout and let my tears run freely.

'This is a cheap and humiliating act of theft,' I tell Santiago, and in revenge I down the glass of wine in one gulp. Over-reacting, he covers his nose. At the same time a photograph of yo-yos tumbles into my cerebral area. In it my brothers are planning a theft from the store of Don Simón, an old man who is almost blind. Crouching behind the door, I eavesdrop on their plan. Then I open the door and tell them I want to go with them because I, too, want a yo-yo.

'You? You're nuts!' says Javier.

'Then I'm going to tell Dad.'

'You do,' threatens Enrique, 'and we'll slit your throat.'

'I'll tell him you said that as well.'

The four of them heave a collective sigh. Alejandro slides his arm around my shoulders and patiently explains that I can't go with them because I'd be sure to end up in gaol. 'Anyway, yo-yos are for boys,' he concludes.

'I want to go.'

They ask me to wait a moment, while they consider my role in the crime. All four join arms and form a circle, with me outside.

'She can't go. She's so stupid. She'll dribble all over the yo-yos.'

'Shut up!' snaps Alejandro. 'She can keep the old man busy while we rip off his yo-yos. She can go in to buy something, and when Don Simón is off guard, we'll grab the yo-yos and take off fast.'

The group breaks up. My brothers come over to where I'm standing, awaiting the results of the discussion.

'You're going to go to Mum,' says Alejandro, giving me the first part of my instructions. 'You're going to ask her if she needs you to run an errand. She's going to say no because you always lose the money. Then you ask her to give you another chance. We all deserve a second chance, don't we?'

I nod my head affirmatively.

It works. My mother looks at me tenderly, smiles, thinks of a possible errand and gives me money to buy a litre of milk. My brothers are waiting for me on the corner, and there I receive part two of my instructions.

Three of us go into the shop. I ask for the milk. When Don Simón wearily turns away to the cooler Javier and Alejandro stuff four yo-yos into their pockets. They still have to get one for me, I notice. Too late! Don Simón is now turned back, his eyes on us. Enrique and Luis whistle from the doorway, gesturing to the street with their eyes. Don Simón gives me the change and, as if I were the owner of all the yo-yos in the world, I pick one up in front of his incredulous eyes and exit after my brothers.

I run to overtake them at the corner.

'Don't run, you idiot. You're going to make him suspicious.'

But already far beyond suspicion Don Simón is yelling curses from the door of his store.

Wearing a woollen jacket and a bowler hat Don Simón barges into the kitchen, up to the table where my father is smoking and drinking coffee while he plays over some celebrated chess games. We can't hear clearly what is being said, only whispers. A chair grates on the floor as my father gets up. His slippers skid over the kitchen floor. He catches us all pretending to play marbles. He lifts me up by one ear. With his dagger-like glare and a raised hand, he tells me to hand over the stolen yo-yo. Terrorized, I confess that it is hidden in the sock drawer.

'Excuse me, sir,' says Don Simón. 'There are five yo-yos missing altogether.'

Alejandro gives the game away by trying to bolt between Don Simón and my father. My father grabs him by the hair on the back of his neck. He gets all five of us in the kitchen and offers Don Simón a cup of coffee. Each one of us stands there with a yo-yo, its string attached to a finger.

'I want you all to play with them,' orders my father. Javier goes first. He drops his yo-yo towards the floor and it dangles there, refusing to return. My father twists his ear viciously.

'Next!'

We all quake.

None of us can work the yo-yo. My father pays Don Simón for all five and apologizes to him. When Don Simón leaves we spend long hours in the kitchen under my father's eye, learning in between pinches and yanks of the ear how to manipulate a yo-yo. When we have mastered it he confiscates the lot.

'I'll buy you a ticket to Bogotá,' offers Cuco.

'No, no,' answers Santiago on my behalf. 'That would be far too expensive. I plan to go to London by bus and fly from there. That way it's a lot cheaper.' Santiago is incapable of concealing his constitutional stinginess. But that doesn't stop him from adding, 'I'll need it in cash.'

That night I was convinced our attempt to extort money from Cuco had failed. But the next day he called. It was the only call of his I ever accepted. We went out one more time. He put the money right into my hands. He caressed me, then had to stop the car to cough all over the steering-wheel. He spat gobs of phlegm out of the window. He also presented me with a card. Through the thin white envelope I could see it was blazoned with a gigantic heart. Back in my room I opened it. Inside the card were another six hundred dollars in freshly minted notes, crisp, uncreased and new-smelling. Printed on the card itself was some joke about lovers told by a cartoon bear. Under it Cuco had written, 'So that you can come back.'

'You've cost him more than a French-style tart!' Santiago sneers, but at the same time he jumps with joy, because we now have twelve hundred dollars to get us out of Spain.

Then remorse set in. I felt the urge to phone Cuco and tell him the truth.

'What truth?' Santiago wanted to know. 'That Interpol is on our trail because of a letter from your mother? That we are locked in a cupboard and can't escape? That we have a dream to realize? That a psychiatrist is on the point of stuffing us full of pills? That everybody at the San Lorenzo eyes you with suspicion and scampers out of the kitchen the second you emerge from your room? That you've lost your job?'

I set myself the task of scanning mental images of prostitutes. One of them refers directly to me when I was in grade nine, a short while before my suicide attempt.

Since I had been unable to grasp the logic of humanity I needed in order to survive in society and had learned nothing from my earlier brush with Felicitas, I decided to make sure that nobody else learned anything.

I had persuaded myself that none of my classmates felt the least interest in chemistry, history or maths. I used to jab them in the ribs with pencils, I passed them scribbled notes, I scratched the covers of their exercise books, and I offered them my shoe to smell. Once in geography class, while the teacher was telling us about Africa, I got up from my desk and danced around, swaying my body in African style, while the more mischievous students beat a tom-tom rhythm on their desks. This minor deviation from academic seriousness was enough to earn me the ill will of the teacher. This was how my clumsy rebellion began, and two days later it ended in an absurd bet.

'I bet you daren't go into the boys' bog and do your African dance there!'

Now that was what I called an academic challenge. The bets piled up. At break-time a mob of classmates followed me to the entrance of the boys' lavatories. Laughter and cheers urged me on. I heard drums beating as my classmates pounded on the door and in I danced, in front of the horrified boys peeing into the urinals.

My mother was summoned to the school. 'I suppose', she purred, 'they want to congratulate me again.' She was accustomed to receiving praise for the scholarly miracles of Lilia.

When I got home the family was in crisis. The geography teacher had exaggerated my sins. She told my mother that I had been dancing naked in front of the boys and that they had rewarded my performance with sweets and fizzy drinks.

My father's punishment went beyond the merely physical. For the next six months he ignored me totally, after telling me that I had his full permission to leave the house and become an exotic dancer. For, as far as he was concerned, I had died.

## 19

My attempts at being honest are over. Santiago is perfectly correct. How long can it have been since even a third-class whore was prepared to have sex with Refugio Vidal? Without knowing it, we performed an act of charity by sleeping with him, and now we had received our just reward. So I went to consult a travel agent. Santiago was thrilled and gleefully checked out posters of Greece, Prague and Thailand.

The woman who handled my enquiry told me the price of a ticket to Bangkok. Six hundred dollars exactly. Santiago was in seventh heaven, organizing and reorganizing the photos to come, but I felt a sudden heaviness in my chest, as if an ice-cube had inserted itself into my aorta and, as it melted, was dripping chilling drops of water into my heart. I collapsed into the chair in front of the agent's desk. Her mouth kept on moving at me, but I heard nothing. Then another character entered this silent movie: a man. He tapped me on the forehead, opened my eyelids with his fingers and breathed on to my pupils. The agent was fanning me with something. The man grasped my hand and spoke to me. His mouth appeared like a gigantic red tunnel into which I was falling, falling. I tried to grab on to his uvula but I went sliding down into the darkness of his trachea. It was there that I bumped into Santiago.

Santiago, I discovered, is flesh without bone. His single eye is a throbbing spiral of flesh, pumping blood. He is like a marble made out of liver, with red slimy extremities. His mouth is a mere pin-prick. We stared at each other for a long time.

Then he speeded up the pulse that activates his blob of a body, and at each beat he emitted a black fog that obscured my vision. I let out a shriek and scrambled up a mound of gooey pulp that rose mountain-like beside him. He raced up after me. I thought my head was going to explode. He grabbed me by the legs to pull me back down. I managed to struggle to the top but only to slip back down. We both ended up in a pool of pus, in which were floating, half submerged, old videotapes covered with green slime. I waded through the pool, ignoring photos that drifted to the banks. I reached the edge and clambered out, but Santiago's body had sunk below the surface as he swam around trying to salvage his precious images. Then I crawled up towards a mass of ashen veins and in under the darkness of its tangled network. There I stayed, as motionless as a hibernating reptile.

Finally I dared to call out, 'Mina! Mina!'

The deep well of blackness responded by assuming a bluish hue. Santiago immediately sounded the alarm. Out of his mouth he launched gasps of blood-red breath that crashed into the abyss and, as they fell, crystallized into violet-coloured quartzes.

I could not move away to escape his rage. All around was the directionless void and cold devastation.

But, to my delight, the blue-black of the distance began turning indigo, as if Mina were answering my call.

Then, abruptly, the man in the silent movie was shaking my body. I finally reacted. I jumped out of the chair and fled from the travel agent's as fast as my legs would carry me.

## 20

Two days later I was on a ferry heading across the English Channel. I felt as light as air. Space and time were under my control. The sea was just the sea. The prow of the ferry was nothing but the prow of the ferry. The sailors were simply sailors. And the coffee-dispensing machine was exactly that. My only luggage was my handbag, which contained my passport and Cuco's money.

I simply don't know how many days I wandered the streets of London. I assimilated myself to its geography without forming memories and composing photographic images. I was London's damp, chilly air, its domes, the waiter who served me, the body that cheerfully ate the food he served. I was the bell that tinkled as I left the restaurant, the steam rising from coffee in a disposable cup, the waves driven to shore by a cruise along the Thames, then a bench and the body seated on it. My shoes looked tatty. I breathed hard between my hands to warm them.

I ended up on Albert Street, a deserted thoroughfare flanked by abandoned houses and derelict sites. There I approached a group of men who were smoking and drinking booze around a fire. I was sure I was already part of them. I sidled into their circle. Silence fell immediately. I was wearing a grin that had not left my face since I had escaped from my closet-room. One of the men pulled out a black package that contained a perfume and offered to sell it to me. I took hold of the box and stroked it. Then I pulled out the bottle and sprayed them all. The owner of the perfume let out a yell of rage. He snatched back the box and bottle and, cursing me, stowed them away inside his clothing.

'You off your trolley, or what?'

I suppose I looked like I might be with my painfully fixed smile.

'Hey, I'm talking to you!' He blew his stinking breath into my face and gave me a push.

'Go on! Piss off!'

But I couldn't move. I was drawn magnetically to their circle and their fire. Perhaps it was the fire more than anything, for my eyes were dripping tears from the cold November weather, even though my grin remained in place.

The man with the perfume spotted my handbag and wrenched it from me. Refugio's dollars were no longer in it; they were hidden inside my shoe. The man up-ended the bag and shook out my passport on to the cobbles. He peered at it curiously.

'You don't speak English? Bloody foreigners!'

He grabbed my arm and pulled me about ten yards out of the circle. He pushed me again and threw my bag and passport at me. 'That means fuck off!'

Some of the men laughed, but I stayed just where I was, for how long I'm not sure. Then the lights went out in the corner shop at the far end of the street. A few figures flitted past us in the dark. All that remained of the fire was a small heap of bright-red coals. The men began to drift away. Of the last two to go, one came back. I watched his silhouette drawing closer. My heart leaped with joy at his approach.

'Mina,' I whispered. It seemed that finally I had found her, as shapeless as a metallic-blue mist seeking to escape from a bottle and spread itself over city after city. The figure reached my body. Out from the centre of blues overlaid with blues stepped Reginald.

'Come with me.'

He took my arm and we walked down the deserted streets. We arrived at a dark house. He pulled a bunch of keys from his coat pocket. He opened a metal gate and we went down steps. He then opened the door of a basement where the ceiling seemed menacingly low because of the unpainted pipes criss-crossing it.

The living space was very small. The place was cold and untidy.

In one corner was a single bed, heaped with woollen blankets.

Reginald switched on a lamp. We looked at each other directly for the first time. He could not have been more than eighteen. While I observed him he put his hands to my cheeks, trying to massage away my ghastly fixed grin. I had hoped to find him still wrapped in the blue mist, but the only blue about him was in the wordless warmth of his two eyes, like a pair of blue marbles.

'What's your name?'

I wanted to answer him, but the words would not come out.

'Me,' he said, pointing to his chest. 'My name is Reginald, Re-gi-nald. Right?'

Finally he had got rid of my smile. I had such a pain in my jaw that even though I wanted to say something I could not articulate a word.

'Come 'ere,' he said. He gestured to me to follow him. He opened a narrow door.

'Bar-froom. Show-er.' He turned a tap on and let the water run. ''O' wa'er. OK?'

Again he took my hand and led me to another corner. He clicked on a light bulb hanging from an enormous pipe. Under it I saw a small refrigerator and an electric cooker. He put water in a kettle. Every time he looked at me he smiled. I felt welcome.

Classes were over. He stopped insisting on knowing my name and trying to teach me things. We drank our tea in silence and ate bread and butter. We slept in the same bed, fully clothed, with our shoes on. He lent me a woollen cap, putting it on my head and pulling it down over my ears. He was still smiling.

At first I didn't speak because I couldn't. Then silence proved an advantage. Our relationship was founded on silence. We drank our tea and ate our bread and butter without a word. The silence forestalled invasions by Santiago. But my smiling certainty that I knew precisely where I was in the world I owed solely to Santiago, and in his absence I succumbed little by little, in early December, to melancholy. This was not a particularly painful experience – because I did not understand what was making me feel so scattered and anxious – so I accepted it as if a telescope were extending itself out of my heart and looking out longingly through the tiny window of the basement up towards the blue beyond.

Reginald had some sort of job. Maybe as a bricklayer or a car mechanic or a plumber. The nights set in early, and he would arrive at the basement, drink his tea, eat a snack and look at me long and tenderly. He would try to teach me some basic English – for example, 'muck under me fingernails', while he was cleaning his nails with a toothpick. He strummed his guitar and sang in a barely audible voice, as if he were afraid I would hear him. I recall him with his eyes shut, displaying the dark line of his lashes. His cheeks would flush when I sat close to him to hear his song. A faint dusky down grew on his chin and upper lip. His fingers were strong and stiff, his nails black. He sang songs about heartbreak, loneliness, politics and war.

I made a habit of sleeping in late. I would get up, make the bed and wash the few plates in the hand basin. To kill time I used to go out in the afternoons. I had become obsessed with numbers. I started by counting my steps down long, busy roads. I made a note of them in a little notebook that Reginald had given me. With an uncertain hand like that of a child at infant school he had drawn the letters of the alphabet and, spluttering with giggles, he sang them out for me to imitate. Finally he admitted defeat. Our language of glances was all we needed. Like a seed germinating in the humidity of the basement, this language without words fed his body and mine. The dizziness and gloom I had felt in the early days of December began to dissipate.

I counted my steps to my regular destination along the road and reached the number 1,850. That was too many. I felt that the number should have been 1,632. Neither more nor less. On my third attempt, taking longer strides, I made it in exactly that number.

My next objective concerned the numbers on private houses and public businesses. Some places did not have their street numbers visible, so I had to go into shops and blocks of flats and ask for them. Nobody questioned my exhausting and exhaustive task. I wore some of Reginald's clothes, the old workman's boots he stored under the bed and his blue woollen cap. Everybody answered me with the seriousness appropriate to a census. Some housewives complained to me about the postman or the government, and with a grave face I jotted down their complaints in my notebook. I nodded courteously as I left and stuck my pencil behind my ear. When the cold weather got too much for me I would hurry back to the basement. With spectacular precision I would count the rooftops, the dark ones, the greens and the reds. Then the awnings. After them, the restaurants, Italian, Chinese and Indian. After them, the neon signs. And I would note the exact time I passed Albert Street on each occasion.

One day I stationed myself at the mouth of the Underground. People came bustling out in great haste, but I would pursue them with my questions.

'Excuse me. We are conducting a survey on the difficulties of being human. What is your opinion of the void?'

'The what?' some would answer.

'Say that again,' said others.

Most of them ignored me or shook their heads at me without slackening their pace. I discovered there were lots of Lilias in London. These always knew what to reply. They came along, impeccably dressed in dark raincoats, with umbrellas that matched their shoes.

'Hmmm!' they would mutter thoughtfully. 'That's a tough one. The void, eh? Well, for me, it's a hole in my stomach.'

When couples were asked, they tended to burst into laughter.

'It's infertility.'

'Death.'

'Loneliness.'

'Rejection.'

'Explain yourself,' said one woman in particular. 'Oh, I see. Well, the void is something we need to make understanding possible. You are there, I am here. If there was no void between us, you know, no space, then I wouldn't be able to see you, would I?'

Then she vanished into her umbrella. I was so taken by her remark that I followed her without her seeing me. She was tall, slender and middle-aged. Her umbrella did not match her outfit. She went inside a building where the walls were all glass. I waited outside for her, and in the meantime I counted how many shoes, black, brown or blue, went by me along the pavement.

It began to get dark, and still she did not emerge from the building. It wasn't to my advantage that Reginald should discover I was leaving the basement: that would have been almost as bad as his finding out I could speak.

When I got back he was already there. He looked at me with a disturbing twinkle in his eye, and then he spoke my name. I realized at once that he had ferreted through my handbag and found my passport. At that moment something in me snapped shut, like a clam trapping an intruding finger inside itself, a finger like the one Reginald used to stroke my teeth.

With his burning lips he tried to warm up my icy cheeks, my forehead and the tip of my nose. In order to distract him I took him by the hand and led him to the little stove. I put the kettle on. We had hard-boiled eggs for supper, but now there was something different in the way he looked at me. His smile resembled my grin when I first met him. There was a fixed quality to it that spoke of inevitable grief.

When supper was over he played his guitar for a brief while, and I took this opportunity to get into the bed, slipping under the blankets, still wearing my cap, scarf, boots and all. He switched off the light and got into the bed beside me. I could hear his agitated

breathing. In the darkness he spoke my name again. He pronounced it as if it were something strange and profound, as
though he were using it to dig under mounds of rubble in search
of Santiago. Inside me, my veins and arteries felt like they were
conspiring against my heart, and it began to beat irregularly.

He ran a finger over my ear nervously like somebody testing
the edge of a razor blade. My mind was concentrating on my numbers, on my census, on the woman from the Underground. He put
his head on my shoulder when he realized I was still awake. Then
once again he spoke my name. I fought it off by trying to recall
every step I took down the avenue. I heard him sigh, and he turned
his body away. Within a few minutes his breathing became regular,
while I was struggling for breath.

Every time I gasped for air Santiago proceeded to reconstitute
himself. The melancholy telescope in my heart was shattered to
fragments, and my connection with the blue beyond was broken.
Suddenly the whole world was jammed inside my brain, wrapped
up tight, with no way to turn it around, not even a little, and so
unlock my memory. A glimpse that escaped through my eyes
allowed me to recognize, in the glow of the sodium streetlights fil-
tering in through the high window, that I was lying there under the
plumbing pipes in Reginald's basement.

Fighting for breath, I got up from the bed and stumbled
around my unlit cage from one side to the other, until I dragged a
chair up under the window and stood on it to peer out. Outside, a
damp mist was drifting listlessly around the lamppost. There I
stayed, fascinated by the mist's movements: it, at least, was not
motionless.

When the alarm clock sounded, Reginald sat up in bed. He
switched on the lamp and saw me still standing on the chair under
the window.

'What's up?' His voice was locked in the frozen world. 'You
OK?'

He reached for my hand and tried to pull me off the chair which, for me, was no longer a chair but my last point of balance on a precipitous cliff. I refused to fall. He shook the chair and caused me to wobble perilously. With both hands I hung on tight to the window-sill.

Then he darted off to the bathroom. By the time he emerged day had dawned. Its pale light fell directly on the road above, which was filling up with cars and umbrellas.

Again his two hands seized my waist. He pulled me off the chair, sat me down on it and crouched in front of me.

He left me there when he went off to work, sitting on the chair, looking after him, with a steaming cup of tea in my hands. Many hours slipped by before I remembered that I had important work to do with my numbers and questions. I dashed out like somebody late for her job. The morning mist had blown away to be replaced by a cheerless sun, light without heat.

At the mouth of the Underground I waited for the woman. Perhaps she would know how to get this huge clod of earth out of my head and how to create the distance necessary for me to observe her as a being outside myself. I couldn't remember her face, but I had a clear idea of her body from behind, the unstylish combination of her clothes and the way she walked. I leaned up against the wall of a shop and checked out the backs of all the women. Then there she was! She was walking faster than anybody else, and I was forced to run to keep up with her. I didn't dare speak to her. Once again she went inside the glass building and once again I sat on the pavement to wait for her. I planned what I would say to her. I would invite her to supper.

Night fell once more. The building seemed to be composed of deceitful mirrors. People went in but nobody ever came out. Then I discovered that there was an exit into the street that ran parallel to the Underground. I crossed the foyer and came out of the rear door.

There I found Santiago waiting for me with a photo he had just taken of the Christmas lights adorning the streets. Everything now had an icy glitter to it, the silhouettes, the cars, the glaring commercial signs. The cold air froze my face and I half closed my eyelids to protect my eyes.

Suddenly, instead of car lights I saw coming towards me the lighted lanterns of a Mexican Christmas procession. At its head staggered my Aunt Socorro, her shoulders drooping under the weight of the empty manger of Jesus and the statues of Joseph and Mary awaiting the miraculous birth. Behind her walked my siblings, behind them the Gonzalez brood – Christmas is the season of peace – and behind them other kids from the neighbourhood singing carols that Aunt Socorro was leading with her strident nasal voice. A car horn blared.

I love processions. Now Aunt Socorro forces us to walk street after street to reach the mysterious house where we will act out our Christmas ritual. We cluster around her while she asks if there is any room for Joseph and Mary. I, too, join in the singing and allow drops of freezing rain to land on my tongue. A harsh ritual rebuff comes from the house. Finally, an accord is reached, and we holy pilgrims are allowed to enter. Then begins the torture of prayer. Down on our knees, we offer thanks that the Divine Word has been incarnated among us. The prayers are endless. The tarmac of the London street is wet.

My rosary beads turn into light bulbs that seem to chase each other around and around a chemist's sign. My eyes focus on the roof-top of the house that offered lodging to the Saviour's mother-to-be. I look around at the faces of adults and despairing children. But out here there is no sheltering roof, no consoling moon. The sky has overwhelmed the street with a shower of murky hail. Turning my head, I notice stairs going up to a second floor. It must be the home of wealthy people, for everything is gilded: the candelabra, the banisters, the numbers on the door. At long last we arrive at the songs of joy and we imitate the sound of tambourines by clapping our hands. Then the warm chocolate in my hands turns out to be cold mud. The cake with the crown and sickly masses of green, white and blue marzipan transforms itself into a policeman who interrupts my prayers. He hurts me as he tries to lift me to my feet.

'I'm fine,' I tell him, wriggling free of his grip. I walk away rapidly in the direction of the basement. It's not too late, I realize, to get there before Reginald. People are still hurrying out of the tall buildings, pushing against each other in a vain attempt to make haste.

I go past the end of Albert Street. There is Reginald, next to the fire, drinking with his friends. He will be getting home late tonight.

## 21

'We will all be late getting home,' declares the voice of Santiago in my ear. I have put the kettle on and removed my clothes to dry them near the little stove. To thwart Santiago I start to count in multiples of five.

'He's a good lad, this Reginald,' continues Santiago. 'The problem is this dump of a basement. And that business tonight out there was, frankly, suicidal. It's one thing to see images and quite another to act them out in the middle of a street in central London.'

I listen to his nagging while I put on Reginald's sweater and socks.

'This kind of thing will be the end of us. I've had enough. I concede that our travel plans were a trifle over-ambitious. I also think we've been striving for far too much in life, but don't forget that striving hard is one way to keep madness at bay.'

I listen as I drink the tea.

'So it's over. Let's head back home. We could carry on with our studies there and go on real-life pilgrimages. We can carry a little lantern behind a flock of people who are singing hymns of praise to the Virgin Mary. We could enjoy a tasty meal with your mother. Let's have no more of this nonsense about eating bread and butter and drinking tea. This obsession of yours with numbers is quite intolerable. You're never going to find that woman you're looking for. Let me draw you a picture of what your life will be like if you stay here. Reginald will tire of you. And there'll be no more hand-outs from Cuco to get you home.'

So that's the way it is, I think. One blackmail after another. The fear of living outside language.

I fall asleep before Reginald gets home. I don't want him

listening to Santiago. The next morning, after Reginald has left for work, I put on my own clothes, even though they are still only half dry.

I leave Reginald a letter. I set out, determined to cross the ocean.

## 22

After a flight, a stopover, another flight and long periods of hanging around in airports my separation from Santiago is over. Once more I have succumbed to the security of a perspective that is unreal and to his interpretations of space. Photographs are spread out to dry on my encephalic bumps and there they acquire an ochre hue. Promises of a brilliant future are tied to my submitting to reality; they are fettered to the rules and regulations of healthy living. The magic of the word is made flesh in a marble-sized creature composed of liver, with all its fantastic abracadabra.

Talking of magic, here is a magic trick I learned from my brother Luis. One day, while my parents are out, probably shopping, he lights a ring on the cooker. He heats up a fork until it is red-hot. Then he pronounces magic words and plunges the fork into a beaker of water. Clouds of steam hiss upwards. Then he slaps the fork down on Lilia's bare arm. She screams, but the fork is inexplicably cold. We all laugh. We beg him to do it again. But Luis bores quickly and prefers to hang out with his friends on the street corner.

I leave the house, deeply impressed by the incandescent coldness of the metal fork. I race down several streets until I get to the house of Martha, my one friend at school. I tell her I had a visit from a strange man in a turban and cloak. He taught me how to turn myself invisible but I don't dare do it in front of her, because she would be sure to faint. Still, I do have another trick to show her. I need fire and a fork to perform it. We go to the stove in the kitchen. We light the gas. I put the tines of the fork in the flame until they turn red, and then I put the fork on Martha's forearm near her wrist. She screams just like Lilia. But then she weeps and weeps and blows on the burn. Her mother bursts in and calls me nasty names. Martha is forbidden to associate with me ever again. So goodbye juices and baked ham at break-times. I return home, picking up pebbles and batting them with a stick. I still can't figure out where the trick went wrong.

'The idiot forgot to put the fork in water!' I am hearing Luis's laughter for the first time in many years.

He is recalling the incident at a party in Lilia's garden. It is my welcome-home party. They have all come to see me. A couple of nephews have been born in my absence, and they are displayed like trophies. Here nothing has gone amiss, for nothing has happened. My mother smiles at what we say, although she doesn't listen to it.

'Do you remember how her mother came to our house to complain? She was like a raging lioness!'

Of course. Now comes the photo of the long-expected end to the misfired trick. My father learns of my blunder and has me brought into the kitchen. There he is seated like a king on a throne, a towel wound around his head like a turban. An empty bucket stands at his feet.

'Kneel down,' he commands. He has a vicious-looking knife in his hands.

I kneel.

'Bend your head over the bucket! I'm going to teach you a trick I know. I hope it doesn't go wrong like yours did.'

I stare down at the bottom of the bucket and my long hair falls forwards over my face. My father begins to saw at my bared neck. He is using the sharp knife but only the blunt edge, as I learn later. I pray to God his trick won't fail.

Other similar images rise from my brother's memories.

We recall the yo-yos that Santa Claus brought one Christmas and old Don Simón. As we reminisce, we drink beer and offer toasts, but a sudden silence falls when the harsh exposure to language peels the glamour off our nostalgic ramblings.

I think about Santiago, and my body feels it is back in that clammy basement, listening to a guitar, while I am counting footsteps and awnings. Now I am listening to Reginald's irregular breathing. Over and over I review the words of the letter I left him. Without warning, an explosion of laughter erupts from my chest, every tone of laughter, choking, fluid, grating, deafening, rich in tears.

## 23

Laughter. Gusts of cackling mirth burst out of my chest uninvited. I had discovered that red-painted lips are the formula for unending laughter. Lipstick is now the instrument I use to recapture the laughter I enjoyed before Santiago's arrival, a harsh, hopeless laughter that shatters the Muzak of daily life, peevishly bringing down the roof on the people close to me.

When I reached fourteen, my laughter began to wither away, for I could no longer copy those around me and had to face the world wearing my own authenticity. Laughter distorted my face, as the creases of my mouth tried to link up with the corners of my drooping eyelids. Laughter I could not contain in the presence of teachers and other authority figures. Laughter I could not carry with me across the world, for it collapsed into silence when I saw myself in the mirror of the void, that suffocating emptiness where no echoes exist, for the invisible atoms and molecules refuse to allow passage to the sound-waves of mirth. That bitter mirth, which contained every ounce of my unhappiness, of my rejection of all I had learned in my fourteen years. The edges of my heart turned to stone under its pressure, taking on the grey, sad colour of lava that regrets ever having left the earth's interior in order to glimpse the light of day.

But my laughter had now returned. It lodged itself like broken glass in my throat. I cannot explain the physiology of laughter, but I know that everything comes gliding up the slippery slope of the larynx, everything I used to be and that I am, to go skidding away before it lands in a heap on the ears of others, like panicky schoolgirls tumbling over each other on an icy pavement.

This hurtful laughter filled out the void left by the loss of Mina. Now no more remains of her than a nostalgia for my beginnings. My breakdown, the dreams shattered by my suicide attempt, the melancholy telescope scanning the blue beyond for some trace of Mina, my journeyings around and around in circles in search of nothing in particular, these are all recorded by Santiago, that creature of the word.

Once we were a single unified being. Then language designed a miraculous link between feelings and thoughts. After that, everything had to struggle across the battleground of cold logic. If an occasional glance, thoughtlessly absorbed in the twilight, chanced to open a crack in this logic, a nervous laugh would promptly seal it.

There followed a decade of truce. Throughout this period my public persona, ever more seductive, was channelled into harmony. It so balanced out my laughter that both currents ran together in a tranquil stream, where I and Santiago flowed side by side. Once my humanity had been a precarious, fragmented gesture, but now it was stabilized by the kindly arts of forgiveness and interchange. It was at this point that Lucio, my jigsaw-puzzle man, appeared, composed of three pieces: the tenderness of Reginald, the generosity of Cuco and the intelligence of Vicente.

Optimistic because of the truce we were taking for granted, we married Lucio. As was to be expected, ten years of inactivity were to prove too much for Santiago. One day, while Lucio was nodding off over his book and I was gazing pensively at the stains on the ceiling of our house, I heard once again the cavernous voice that had been silent for so long.

'This man is an incubus.'

'He is the man who loves me.'

'I can't believe that.' His voice was now childish. 'Haven't you noticed how he takes everything you have to offer? He's put an end to plans and dreams.' I did not understand to what plans and dreams he was referring. Most likely, Santiago sketched out ideas and maps on the soft surface of the tank of pus he dwelt in. 'When you're asleep, he puts his nose near your mouth and inhales your breath. That's how he survives. It's nothing new for him to tell you how well he is feeling. You, on the other hand, are frozen there like a pillar of salt in front of the television set. His semen is lava. It hardens as it builds up inside your bloated womb!'

'That's my colitis!'

'No, it's feelings you're not supposed to be feeling. There's a pillar of cement growing in there. Soon you'll be all cement. Check him out carefully. There's nothing behind his eyes. Look into the pupils and you'll see right down into the abyss. When he comes close, the marks of what makes a human being human go all blurry. What does he offer you in return for all the vital juices he squeezes out of you?'

'For one thing, protection.'

'So that's it. The big con.'

'I've never felt so safe in my life.'

'Safe? Safe from what?' Then he added, 'I asked you a simple question: what does he offer you in return for all the life he sucks out of you?'

'He understands me. He understands everything. He brings me breakfast in bed. He is a good man.'

Santiago let loose a sinister chuckle. 'It suits him to behave well.'

'I don't want to discuss the matter any further.' I got up from my armchair and headed to the refrigerator.

'Oh, brilliant! Let's eat! That'll solve everything.'

'I didn't have any pudding.'

'Let's silence the truth with our nutritional needs. Is that your answer? You distract yourself with a couple of simple pleasures while the man is eating you alive. Let me tell you something. Hey, that bun you picked up has a strawberry-jam filling! I'll tell you why he picked you. He saw a woman out of sync with reality, whose only defence was an ambiguous smile nobody could figure out.'

'I don't know how to smile,' I retorted, chewing away. 'Lilia is the one who knows how to smile.' But then I recalled the smile that had been stuck on my face on the ferry to England.

'Don't know how to smile?' Santiago took advantage of my error to sneer at me. 'You're a woman who collects false memories the way other people collect paintings.'

I switched on the coffee-pot and toasted another bun. The afternoon sun was slamming down through the kitchen door.

'You're not going to convince me. He's a good man.'

'If he is, why didn't he choose a good woman like your sister?'

My saliva began to acquire a bitter, metallic taste. Instead of eating jam I felt I was sucking on a rotten grapefruit.

Santiago kept on talking and I began to chant childishly:

> I don't hear nothing,
> I don't hear good,
> Because my ears
> Are made of wood!

He pulled out a freshly developed photo.

'Check this out,' he said, shaking the image to dry it off. 'Here comes the monster!'

In it we are celebrating the birthday of a colleague who works with me at the translation agency.

'Why did they invite you?' Santiago wanted to know. 'Because you're such a lively, enthusiastic little soul? Or maybe because you say hi to her every morning when she comes in to work?'

'This can't be happening,' I said. I switched off the coffee-pot and looked in the pantry for a bottle of wine. When I tried to pull the cork out it came to pieces.

'I'm going to tell you why they invited you.' He pulled out from deep down in his collection an image in black and white. Lucio was still asleep in his armchair with an open book on his lap, but in the image he approaches wearing a cloak and dark sunglasses. He is staring in the direction of my office. Night is falling.

'That's a picture of Dracula!' I said, with a giggle. And at that moment I managed to get the rest of the cork out of the bottle.

'Well, everybody looks alike in the dark. But see how he is staring at you. Now night has fallen and he removes the sunglasses. You, in contrast, remain fully illuminated by the lights in your cubicle.'

I poured myself a full glass and took a big swallow.

'You're the evil one,' I told him. 'You're a devil. Disappear!'

I got up and put on some music to wake Lucio.

Santiago spoke his last words of the day. 'That's why you're always so tired and are always getting infections in your bodily fluids. Every morning it's more of a struggle to get out of bed. The garden needs watering. Your dog has run away. Your cat died. The house is overrun by ants. This place is turning into a coffin, wouldn't you say?'

# 24

The following morning I got out of bed, determined to take control of the situation. Yes, it was true that the house was crumbling to pieces. Just to think of Lilia's lovely home sent me scrambling to the telephone to call in the help of an interior decorator. They brought samples to my office. I chose a red and gold wallpaper for our bedroom. I made several phone calls in search of a reliable gardener. When Lucio picked me up from work I asked him to take me to the pet shop. We arrived back home with an Alsatian puppy and two budgerigars.

Santiago showed up, full of sarcasm, as I was fitting a sheet of newspaper into the bottom of the birdcage.

'Tweet, tweet, tweet!' he mocked. 'I see you've solved all your problems.'

I ignored him for as long as I could.

Lucio was outside fixing something.

'Tweet! The woman who falls to pieces in a crisis, tweet, went out and bought budgies, tweet, tweet.'

I tried to pick up one of the birds to help me ignore him.

'The victim recovers her energy so that the vampire will have more to feed on. She'll turn herself into a juicy morsel the better to satisfy his appetite. If you discover your husband's true identity, who is going to believe you? A priest? Your mother? Oh, I know. The Macho Brigade!'

I thought about my father.

'Of course! I was forgetting the old man. Everything he didn't do for you in life, he can do for you now he's dead!'

Lucio came into the kitchen and planted a kiss on my hair.

'All done!' he said to me, as if I knew what he was talking

about. He washed his hands in the sink. Then he rubbed his fingers hard with the scouring-pad.

What was he washing off?

'Don't worry,' said Santiago. 'An incubus never feels guilty. He likes to make you think he doesn't exist. Then he eats you away, quietly, slowly, exquisitely. By the way, what would you like for supper? As if it mattered!'

As if I were an echo, I said, 'What would you like for supper?'

Instead of Lucio, what looked back at me was a wide tunnel full of foul creatures waiting for me to fall asleep.

We ate our supper in silence. Lucio kept smiling. His teeth now had the look of fangs. That night I couldn't sleep. I sat on the edge of the bed and scrutinized him in the darkness. I ended up seeing him as a gargoyle curled up in the foetal position, a gargoyle that snored.

I came up with a temporary solution. I would wait until Lucio fell asleep, then I'd creep away into the spare bedroom and lock the door behind me. My mental alarm clock was very precise. It would wake me before dawn and I'd get back into our bed.

Lucio did not notice. He would get up the same as always, bursting with a genial enthusiasm for life. He sang in the shower. He would come out, wrapped in a towel, and fill the whole house with the smell of coffee and the sound of baroque music. This was the signal for me to crawl out of bed.

Santiago undermined this stratagem. 'I warn you he doesn't need physical proximity to finish you off. He can do it at any moment. When he's kissing you, when he's looking at you, while you're lost in some book or other. When he comes up behind you as you're watering the garden.'

He kept up his attacks in my dreams. He employed resources he had never used before, a photograph that had a soundtrack and special effects.

'Look, this is how he is finishing you off.'

In my dream I open my eyes. My vision hurtles dizzyingly around a corner, like a camera loaded on a dolly shooting pictures in the depths of a mine. The truck slows down as I hear phlegmy breathing, a snorting that comes from the insides of a beast. But I see nothing. I am desperate to get out of the cave. I try to run in the direction away from the breathing of the animal, which is now sniffing out my trail. The beast takes a flying leap. Its hide is covered with spines and they rip into my neck. I want to escape its hold. I scream. The beast pins my arms down so that I cannot move.

Lucio was holding me in that position when I woke up. He tried to calm me down by whispering in my ear. 'It was just a bad dream.' But his face was still hidden in my neck, and the bristles on his chin hurt me. I struggled out of his embrace. Instead of seeing the numbers of the digital alarm clock all red, it was Lucio's eyes that burned red. With a frantic leap I was out of the bed.

'Don't come near me!' I shrieked.

Lucio got out of bed and switched on the light. We stared at each other for a second or two. I can't say what he saw in me at that moment. What I saw was a sleepy man wearing blue pyjamas, with an expression on his face that was both weary and puzzled, who was trying to find his glasses.

I was beginning to feel sorry for him, looking so defenceless there, but then I stroked my neck and felt some light scratches there. I shut myself in the bathroom and placed my burning cheek on the cold tiles.

I went skidding forwards unstoppably until I plunged headlong into the memory of my fourteenth year when I was forced to accept the loss of Mina, my marvel of a friend, and face the horrifying prospect of either entering a whirling void or seeing the entire universe compressed into the space of a light bulb. My Mina, she who came to me from the beyond, always fascinated by the music of my urine running hot from me, always ready to test the waters of the ocean. Mina, enamoured of the colour of cockroaches and the rigid skin of a dead rat. Together, on many an afternoon, we crept into my mother's bedroom while she snoozed away the siesta hour and took delirious delight in her enormous-seeming body as we wound an index finger in and out of her capricious curls and kissed her cold bare feet. Back then there was no terror in the approaching footsteps of my father. I was all eyes peering up at the mass of coarse hairs sprouting from his wide nostrils. I stood stupefied by the flexibility of my brothers' bodies as they climbed fences and trees with equal bravado and recklessly charged across swollen rivers. My Mina, soaked by the rains of October or basking like a lizard in the noon-day summer sun. Mina with her goodnight kisses that always tasted new. Mina, lover of things without number: hurricanes, waves, wind, garbage, the dead, old iron, puddles, frogs, sand that burned the soles of the feet, mangoes glowing on their trees, squabbles, experiments, the stink of burning rubber, brightly coloured vehicles racing past the window, the rag-and-bone man who stole away children, Sunday pocket money, the Chinese sweet-seller, a rose-bud opening, drying out and toppling from its stem.

My mother taps on the door. I have been sitting in the bathroom for some time now with my veins opened, but the blood is still coursing through my body. The tapping turns into banging. How much longer, I ask myself, before everything comes to an end? My father is ready to smash the lock. I play with the wounds in my opened wrists. They are like little mouths. With my fingers I force them to pout, to smile, to frown. The blood leaks out with an infuriating slowness.

My father manages to break open the door as I am hit by a current of searing fire that demands I surrender my life to it. It burns its way along the paths of my blood until it finally installs itself in the space behind my forehead.

From this vantage point it forces my eyes open. The invasion is declared a triumph! Everything suddenly shines with a terrifying lucidity. I am filled with a false enthusiasm, and for a moment I mistakenly believe that Mina has been restored to me. But instead, for the first time I hear the voice of Santiago, who then, as now, tells me to get up off the floor.

Lucio also forced the door. I had been in the bathroom far too long without answering him. He crouched down to hug me. But it was my mother's voice I heard.

'Good God in heaven!' she screams. 'The girl wants to kill herself!'

'I can't believe my eyes,' says my father while he lifts me up with one arm and reaches with the other for alcohol and bandages in the medicine cabinet. My mother shakes off her habitual detachment and asks me with a pained grimace, 'But why? Why?'

'What do you mean why?' answers my father. 'She's failing at school. She can't sit down long enough to study. And when she gets home you have her sweeping and mopping the house.'

'She wants to kill herself because I make her clean the house?' asks my mother incredulously.

'What else could it be?'

After a makeshift bit of first aid my father leads me into the kitchen. He puts on some water for coffee and sits down opposite me.

'What you've just done is a total disgrace. If you're set on killing yourself, go and do it somewhere else. Not in this house, got it?'

'Yes.'

He twists his head around to make sure nobody can overhear him and gives me whispered advice on the best ways to kill myself. 'Next time get some sleeping pills and a bottle of tequila. Drink it down along with the pills. If you decide on gas, you'll need to rent a room with a gas fire. You open the tap with one of these things.' He stands up and sorts through his toolbox, looking for the appropriate implement. 'Have you got enough money to rent a room with a gas fire?'

I shake my head.

'Then throw yourself under a train. But you don't do anything in this house, understand?'

Clutched in Lucio's embrace, I discovered traces of skin from my neck under my own fingernails.

Nice try, Santiago! Clever trick!

## 25

In less than two months Santiago put me through a host of wild nightmares. Some of them woke me up, while others pursued me even after I was awake. Once I walked to the window to shake off the after-effects of what had been only a mildly unpleasant dream, and there I saw Lucio out on the rear patio ripping the skin off a human victim. At other times I could not wake at all, for my eyelids were two metal curtains too heavy to raise. At those times Mina availed herself of the complicated geometry of dreams and their instant transformations to elude Santiago and came to my aid and woke me.

That was until Santiago discovered the plumbing system that allowed her to sneak into my dreams. Then, down the strainer of the drain he emptied weird logarithmic formulas that mimicked the gurgling rush of water and barred her access.

Sometimes I think I am conducting a wordless conversation with Mina like those we enjoyed in our earliest days. But she cannot get past the strainer in the pipe and all I hear is a polysyllabic word that sounds like the booming music of the ocean, but in fact Mina is not really there. Deep in my dreams I promise I will set out in search of her, but on waking I succumb to the insistent battering of Santiago. So my Mina remains aloof, unreachable on her starry throne, for ever hoping to win the battle against Santiago and, on descending, to show up daily life for the sham it is.

Then arrives my good-morning kiss from Lucio, fresh from the shower. I am lying face down and his damp hair is cold on my neck. He gives a soft laugh, which I interpret as his embarrassment at having enslaved, as if by divine right, the life of the woman who loves him. But I react with generosity, my standard response. Lucio and I are paragons of generosity. We are generous with our bodies, generous when it comes to giving the benefit of the doubt, generous about conceding spaces. We are tender with the words we address to each other. Lucio behaves courteously towards my depressions, my prolonged silences produced by the cerebral dysfunctions that Santiago induces on a whim. I am generous towards his optimism, his ecological formulas designed to save humanity from catastrophe. I am generous with his aquiline profile, framed by childlike curls that fall on his neck, while he writes letters of support to financially strapped charitable organizations. I am generous towards his memory packed with trivia about the major philosophers who have challenged life to reveal its meaning.

And he is generous towards my failed attempts to be a housewife.

This pact of cordiality arose out of mutual compassion. We are not two people with hearts like empty vessels that can be replenished by an invigorating interchange of intimate bodily fluids. Rather, we are two vessels shattered against life's illusions. We have lost our faith in metaphors and have turned pragmatic and precise to prevent our brittleness from being shattered even more.

We have formed a social union based on an uncomplaining acceptance of the everyday. From time to time, with a sort of panting nostalgia for our lost sexual passions, we sit naked on the patio and drink drops of the falling rain.

All the same, Lucio, like Lilia, bursts with sunny enthusiasm, organizing ability and prosaic methodicalness. I drift along, a pale moon to his efficient sun, one or two steps behind him, when we go for a walk along streets or through parks. That way we are spared the necessity of walking arm in arm and gazing at each other with a permanent smile.

## 26

My smile gets progressively more nervous. The grinning ellipse extends to its maximum reach. But Lucio reacts cordially to my boomerang-shaped mouth. Deep down we are partners in confronting the unnameable, the particles of energy that underlie human life but are alien to it. He preserves his silence about them, to avoid feeding them with the force of his imagination. He asks me no questions about my shivers, my floods of tears. He simply hugs me tight until my fears start to lose their heat.

Santiago avenges this consolation with his own tales of terror.

Nightmares are child's play compared with the stories he tells my wide-awake brain. It is as if we are in a perpetual winter's night, where he sits by the blazing fire of my innermost energies and flips through a book of lurid horror stories. This book, which details the origin of the incubus and the vampire, is not written in any human language because, he tells me, such creatures immediately kill anyone who, even in fantasy, reveals the formulas that bring them to life. But the formula requires a woman like me with a hole in her heart, close to where babies suck their first milk. Inside this hole a swarm of resentments weave the placenta for the womb that bears the incubus.

At any hour of the day Santiago will whisper to me. He answers all my doubts and queries with an enviable complex of logically compelling reasons. Thus, as I get into bed and lie down, I have been taught that under my pierced heart a tunnel opens up through the flesh and leads to a soft landing-place, the spongy earth where consciousness fades away to nothing, and there hangs, its body throbbing fiercely, the dark foetus of the next incubus awaiting birth.

That is why Doña Rosa, Lucio's mother, is an optical illusion, a human-seeming form who sucks the life-energy out of those around her. If anyone visits her house, she forces herself out of her usual comatose state and manages to maintain a lively conversation with the visitor, thanks only to her mechanical reflexes.

Santiago assures me that before long I will end up in a condition similar to hers.

Already I have only to observe how reality recoils from my gaze.

The more coherence Santiago's arguments acquire, the more scrambled become the objects in my sight. The wall, the red traffic signal, the gaping void, a foetus, Lilia, a trip abroad, Reginald, Lucio, all mix their colours in a shapeless mass of undirected rage and nonsensical violence.

## 27

Santiago must be a being independent of my body and my imagination. Otherwise, where am I getting all these stories from? The most heart-breaking story I have in my album concerns a bewildered dog.

I am around eight years old. We are returning from a short vacation and find our house ransacked. The thieves stole such personal belongings as our clothes and an alarm clock, since my family's economic position did not run to our leaving jewellery and seductive electrical appliances around the place. My father was particularly enraged because the thieves had pretty much left him in his underwear, having taken his three pairs of khaki trousers. He went so far as to accuse the postman of the robbery the next time the poor fellow came to drop off the mail wearing khaki trousers. My mother and brothers had to hold him down to stop him removing them.

To prevent a second theft, we got an enormous black guard dog named Baxter. The perplexed creature had already passed through the hands of five owners in four years. We took to him immediately, because after sniffing us out he pranced around wagging his tail in loving delight.

But it took only one brief family holiday for him to get his scents in a muddle. Here is the photo. We are once again returning home late at night, this time after a visit to my mother's parents. My father pulls out his key to open the front door when the air is filled with menacing growls. It is Baxter dutifully defending his territory and baring his powerful teeth to prove it. My father slips his hand through the grating to loosen the padlocked chain. Baxter does not appreciate the intrusion and leaps to bite my father's hand. Only an agile leap backward saves my father from serious injury.

Baxter barks furiously and wakes up the whole neighbour-hood. People begin to emerge from their houses and find my family standing, baffled and thwarted, in the street, barred from entering their own house.

My father strides from one side of the pavement to the other, puffing on a cigarette and cursing vilely. A well-intentioned neigh-bour tries to distract Baxter, while my father makes a second attempt. But Baxter is no fool, and with psychotic energy he whirls back and forth, defending the whole doorway.

Soothing words have no effect on him. Shouts and chunks of sausage tossed by another neighbour fail to impress him. Nothing will deter him from his mistaken sense of duty. Two hours later he is still warding off his enemies. My father throws rocks and lighted matches at him. He threatens to kick him to death. All to no avail.

We go back to Grandma's and spend the rest of the night there. The following morning we return to the house, accompanied by a vet armed with a syringe. The precaution is unnecessary. Baxter welcomes us joyfully, wagging his bushy black tail with undis-guised glee. Extravagant licks from his pink tongue and the humble submission in his black eyes get him nowhere. He is taken away by his seventh owner.

That photo is followed by Santiago's collected images of foul beasts. Some are patently plagiarized from other imaginations, but the most menacing beast, the one created solely out of Sant-iago's fears, is a monster whose strength and cunning are perfectly tailored to carrying out its most perverse fantasies. Its name is Lucio.

# 28

Thanks to something, perhaps to the thin thread that still ties me to Mina, I am aware deep down that I am being misled. But the thread is so tenuous that it cannot hold for long. When it snaps I lose control of reason, of the things I see and hear, of what comes spewing out of my mouth, like venomous foam, against Lucio and others who surround me.

With my will-power lost, I step out into the street and find there a rain that does not wet me. It evaporates as it falls, but it leaves my vision blurry. A fierce wind howls in my ears and horrifies me. Then the sun's hot rays come crashing down like lightning and I have to turn my back on them and hurry home.

When I step out next I am wearing a waterproof overcoat, a sou'wester and tall wellington boots that I bought in case of a flood. From time to time I dare to glance up at the dazzling sky, defying its heat. If I use my imagination sufficiently, I can feel a gentle breeze.

I come across Lucio, walking along entirely unprotected from the sun. Now he is opening the door of his car.

He bows graciously and invites me to get in. As I enter, he pulls off my sou'wester. He opens a paper bag that contains a decent pair of shoes, and he slowly removes my wellington boots. He humours me with a few jocular words.

I want to talk in order to answer him, to tell him about Santiago, to side-step shame for once and cast some light on my problem, to ask for help.

The very thought of receiving help converts the car into Lucio's mobile lair. Now the filthy beast will drive me into unknown territory and abandon my bloodless carcass there, once he has sucked the life out of it.

Lucio parks the car in front of my office. He switches off the engine and offers to take me home, if that is what I want. Pale with shame, I make a great effort to get control of my vision and manage to see the real features of the building and pavement, while Lucio smiles at me, assuring me I am fine.

'Fine? How are you going to be fine?' Santiago asks me in the elevator. 'That creature isn't going to change. That ridiculous get-up was the best you could do with the remnants of instinct he's left you with, but it's not going to deter him. He's still set on annihilating you.'

Then he screams. 'I'm at the end of my tether!'

I put my hands to my ears.

'Let's go,' he urges. 'Let's make a run for it! How can I convince you that your office is full of his accomplices and that some of them are incubi themselves? That's your real tragedy, not listening to me. You think I'm somebody else, but I'm not. That's how you started this whole nightmare, by refusing to admit that I'm only your feeble attempts at reason.'

The gates of hell slide open and there stands the accountant from my office.

'Don't let him inside the lift!' shouts Santiago. 'Press the button. Shut him out.'

The lift doors do not close fast enough, so I whack the man hard on the head with my handbag just as he is stepping inside. He staggers back, and I take advantage of his confusion to press the close button of the lift once more.

In the foyer of the building the doors open again. I stand there, looking out.

I cannot leave without some form of protection.

'You have to get out,' says Santiago.

'I can't walk.'

'Make an effort. We have to get away before they come looking for us.'

I totter forwards, as the waters of a swollen river come pouring into the building. I hang on to some rocks to stop the river from sweeping me away.

'I need my wellington boots,' I say. 'I need my boots.'

I reach the kerb, just where it emerges from the water. I keep my balance and move forwards. I reach the corner. The sun dazzles me, but it doesn't stop me seeing a huge wave lifting itself up in the distance. I swing my arms high to keep my handbag from getting wet.

I cannot help it; everything gets soaked.

We have walked for far too long. It is now well after dark and I take refuge behind some bushes in a deserted square. I remove my clothes and spread them out to dry. I gather together my money, my bank cards and other credentials, as well as my powder-compact and my eye-shadow. Santiago talks and talks, never stopping. I hum a tune to myself until I fall asleep.

# 29

I wake up in a hospital bed. There are no tubes or restraining straps attached to my body. I get up from the bed and drag a chair over to the window, which is divided into tiny squares.

I do not know how long I have been here. I imagine a doctor walking into the room to ask me how I feel, and in walks a doctor. I get off my chair and stare at him. He reads from a file folder in his hands and nods approvingly.

'How are you feeling?'

The predictable question immediately puts Santiago on guard. I hear him firing questions at me, but I know that this is the moment to ignore Santiago and act out my own desires, now or never.

I must look agitated, for the doctor tells me to calm down.

Santiago forces a sigh, but I oblige him to convert it into precise words, an elegant flow of considered language, forgoing all his usual arrogance.

With an acting ability rarely seen before, Santiago mimics Mina's authenticity to perfection. He squeezes every last drop of sweetness out of himself and avoids any mention of floods, of incubi and, above all, of escaping from the hospital.

While Santiago is occupied in deluding the doctor, I slip away into the shadowy areas of the brain. I stand motionless for a while to let my eyes adjust to the uncertain reddish light. Santiago has his back to me, perched on the ocular mechanism from where he playfully directs sight at the doctor, as if toying with a pair of gigantic binoculars.

Something clatters to the ground, and Santiago spins around. I avoid being seen by concealing myself in a darkened recess.

The doctor repeats a question, and this obliges Santiago to crouch down once again over the eyes.

I find myself in front of a small mound of pulsing flesh, swollen like a replica of my badly constipated belly. I climb up it and suddenly hear that Santiago is stuttering, as though treading on this piece of flesh interferes with the flow of language. I slide down the other side towards the tank of pus. Right now not a single photo is floating in the acid-green goo.

As I squelch through the gummy mush, I become aware that Santiago has lost the thread of what he was saying. He must have detected me. If he were less arrogant he would now come charging after me, but I know his pride will not let him lose the battle with the doctor's leading questions. I recognize the uneven ground under the network of veins, both large and small, where once before I was reduced to crawling along. At the end of the tangled tube I find myself on the verge of a precipice. Small bones and strips of calloused flesh litter a mountain pass, but, as I get nearer, they are hidden by a rising mist, at first red, then turning black.

From the far distance comes a hubbub of anxious voices. Thousands of nightmares are hovering there, continually interchanging features, so as to be ready to perform in answer to a summons from Santiago. I feel compassion for the hundreds who will never see the light of dreams, those discouraged and disappointed ghostly images. Flitting about the red-tinted gloom, their shapeless silhouettes make pained gestures at having to reconstitute themselves endlessly in the hope of being called on to play a role in Santiago's capricious theatre.

I look ahead to what I remember was the distance, but now I encounter only the cranial dome, perfectly marked out by its red walls. The fleshy matter here seems repulsively alive.

Suddenly everything falls silent and lets me hear the fury of Santiago, who is shouting, sobbing, pleading. He is still in control of my body, as it wars against the doctor. In the end the doctor wins the day by injecting into Santiago a substance that slams the binoculars shut and paralyses Santiago's puny body until it resembles a statue perched precariously on its little mound.

Dazzled by the abrupt onset of lucidity, I totter along the edge of the tank. Hanging from arteries that protrude from the walls are cocoons containing the larvae of dreams so wild they would baffle the imagination. I break one open, interrupting its gestation. Inside is a viscous paste in which is set a pair of unseeing eyes. I hurl it far away, shuddering at what it might have become.

I need to speed up. I do not know how long the sedative will keep Santiago quiet. I tread carefully, pushing to one side the adipose tissues and the intricate network of blood vessels. I follow the open ground along which Santiago dashes to supply nourishment to his creatures. Turning a corner, I find myself on the threshold of a grotto.

It is Santiago's lair.

Here are catacombs of finely sculpted flesh, an elegant masterpiece, where the sly tenant dwells with all his weird obsessions. On a work table lies a terrifying plan for my next fit of delirium. It contains a map of my brain, with numbered areas and bewildering geometrical patterns. There, charted with precise coordinates, are the routes he navigates.

By the wall, beside the table, stands a delicate construction of cells like a honeycomb. Here the flesh does not throb but is of a pink material as hard as polished marble. I touch it curiously. With nervous care I open one of the cells and am startled to see a black-and-white image of my mother as a teenager. It is night-time and she is running along the bank of an irrigation ditch. A man is pursuing her. He catches hold of her and throws her down on to the soft earth. My scream and hers mingle into one. Her desperation disrupts my heartbeat. I slam the cell shut and open another. Here is another black-and-white photo, this time of my brother Luis. He is staring at the nakedness of his sleeping wife, but he is humiliated by sexual impotence. In another cell I listen to the weeping of my father as a child. He is playing the violin, while rose petals wither on the corpse of my grandmother.

Where on earth did Santiago find such images?

I open more cells: voices, bangs, moons and seas. I close them: cackles of laughter in the distance, the far distance.

One of the cells is throbbing lightly. I look at it curiously. The palpitations are regular and unhurried. I pluck up my courage and open it. A hysterical cloud of colours comes bursting out. Then it dissipates, and I am looking into a long tunnel.

I step inside. Here are memories. I speak to them. I want to touch them, these memories of my siblings, the memories of myself being with them. But they are all holograms. I cannot accept this, and I apologize every time I pass through one.

I trek down a long road. Now, at long last, the reds are turning purple. I sigh, sensing the proximity of Mina. I pick up the sound of her breathing, for ever full and tireless. She feels no resentment for all our lost opportunities. I grasp the hand of her blue body and then I turn my eyes, for a few seconds, to see myself in the hospital bed.

Lucio is sitting beside my sleeping body. From the mouth of the tunnel I reach out and stroke his hair. I beg him not to come back here and witness what is bound to happen, now that Santiago will never speak an intelligible word again.

Lucio lays his cheek on my tranquil breast and says goodbye.